Outlier Man

A Vinnie Briggs Mystery, Volume 1

Charles Puccia

Published by Carduna Publications, 2020.

Also by Charles Puccia

A Vinnie Briggs Mystery
Outlier Man
Detour Man
Salt & Pepper Man

Vinnie Briggs Hot Mystery
Ice Cream Man
Baseball Man

Watch for more at www.charlespuccia.com.

Table of Contents

Outlier Man
Charles Puccia

Outlier Man Copyright © 2017 Charles Puccia
www.charlespuccia.com[1]
Published by Carduna Publications
ePub ISBN: 978-0-9963234-4-4
Paperback ISBN: 978-0-9963234-5-1
Edited by Ben Way (benjaminway.co.uk)
Copy edit and proofreading by Ian Howe
eBook formatting and cover design by FormattingExperts.com

***

If you enjoyed reading *Outlier Man*, please rate this book or leave a review for other readers. It means a lot to me—and to Vinnie, who is busy investigating crimes at BIG, and complicating his relationships with Ben, Dan, and Ginny.

Other books in the Vinnie Briggs Mystery series.

Ice Cream Man

Baseball Man

Thank you!

---

1. http://www.charlespuccia.com

Remember to sign up to my email list at charlespuccia.com for pre-release information on Vinnie's next story. Look for the audiobook versions of VB stories.

Sincerely,

Charles J. Puccia

vbstories2@gmail.com

An Unusual Encounter

Chapter 1

Present Day

Vinnie stared at the murderer's letter as if it was a freshly deposited dog turd. A reminder that he had solved the case; well, he and his team at the Briggs Investigative Group, but it didn't feel like it. They had identified the murderer, prevented further needless deaths, yet everyone was disappointed. In his other cases—admittedly only two—and before he became a licensed New York PI, before he started his Manhattan agency, he had solved the murders. Those cases felt good, identifying the criminals its own reward, better than a client's fee. Now his fee was paid, the murderer identified, and the client satisfied. But not Vinnie.

Holding the letter, sliding the edge between his index finger and thumb, feeling the paper's texture did not satisfy.

Solving the case felt so wrong.

***

Seven Months Earlier

Midway along the hospital ward the man stopped walking. The familiar pungent odor crept up his nostrils while his brain churned as he recalled the assault that resulted in murder. He was disoriented, dazed.

"Roger, that you? I didn't know you heard about Emily. So kind of you to stop by."

"Oh—" Roger blinked, and his emotional befuddlement was obvious as he tried to recognize his former neighbor, Glen Dingle. "Uh, sorry, I didn't... I mean... I'm just dropping this off." Roger lifted a box of chocolates and an envelope as if clarifying his response.

Glen patted Roger's back as if they were still close friends sharing a beer at a barbecue, still cheering their sons on the football team, their wives still teaching colleagues at Lincoln High, and forgetting the shame that had long buried their friendship.

Tugged onward by Glen's hold on his elbow, Roger entered the intensive care room, his eyelids fatigued from blinking. The scene too familiar: a large tube traversed the bedridden woman's throat below two closed blackish-blue patinaed eyes. He blinked again, yet failed to recognize Emily Dingle.

Roger stepped closer, unsure what to say. Should he let Glen in on the cruel joke that sooner or later the machines would stop? Tell him his wife was already dead, only neither she nor Glen knew it? Tell him about the nauseating feeling that would suffuse every cell of his body on agreeing to pull the plug on his wife? This had been Roger two weeks earlier.

He decided this was not the time, not yet. Glen has hope. He'll believe me less than doctors. He doesn't care about electrical brain activity. Let him hope for a few days more. Ha. He'll soon hate the nurses and doctors for... what did they say to me? *Mr. Bryant, people react differently... take time to let it sink in... it's your decision, but your wife is...*

Roger looked at his outstretched hand with the chocolate box and gift certificate thank-you he brought for the nursing staff. That day could not be scrubbed away. Roger yelled at the nurses. Cursed and criticized them. Insisted they knew nothing, and that his wife would recover. The nurses tutted, patronized: "We understand, Mr. Bryant. Take your time. It's your decision." He fumed until the day he accepted the medical team's diagnosis. Alice would not recover because she was already dead.

With his sixteen-year-old son Ken, thirteen-year-old daughter Katy, and Alice's mother and sister they huddled waiting for the silence. The hush was brief, broken by their collective wail. The day Alice officially died the family ceased to care about each other.

No, thought Roger, *I'll not be Glen's prophet... what was that sonnet read at Alice's funeral...? Thy end is truth's and beauty's doom and date.* Roger looked from Emily to Glen. Different people take different amounts of time to process bad news.

"Why are you here if you didn't know about Emily?"

Yes, why? Roger mumbled about thanking the nurses. He told Glen of Alice's early retirement at fifty; her celebration with colleagues; her call around ten that awful night to say she would fill the car and pick up a few items for the weekend at their Jersey Shore cottage. Roger's lips widened as he repeated his oft-told quip that Alice counted groceries like a five-year-old. His smile dissipated as he recalled the midnight knock at the door—two men, porcelain faces lit by the outdoor lamp, hats in one hand, the other pushing metal badges forward like lances. Talk of a metal object and a beating. An offer to escort him to the hospital.

"Geez, Roger, I'm so sorry. I had no idea. It wasn't in the local paper... well, it wouldn't, would it, since you moved away. Big house in Ridgewood, right?"

Roger looked at Glen sitting at his guard-like bedside chair and realized he had never liked him. Emily he could take or leave. Did he dislike Glen for his lack of ambition? He abandoned the Big Apple competition to start his two-man New Jersey firm, minuscule compared to Roger's financial group on Madison Avenue and Sixtieth Street. It was no secret Roger's earnings tripled Glen's, and it explained why Glen struggled to make ends meet.

Or maybe his dislike for Glen came after he had no choice but move his family to the *big* house, the upper-income neighborhood, not that Roger didn't appreciate the prestige. But everyone knew the Bryant family didn't move for a better zip code, Glen more than most. Roger rewrote history to include that he never liked Glen.

The machine hummed in the background, blending Emily into the conversation. Roger listened. Emily never blended. She bellowed louder than the men; interrupted people during barbecues; energetically organized the women's snack roster for Little League and Pop Warner games; and chaired the parents' booster club for Lincoln High School football when their sons Ken and Brett were still teammates.

Roger's lips twisted. The families lost touch. They knew why. Were they ever really close or just friends by proximity made strangers by the event? Roger looked at the battered Emily. Did she and his Alice have more in common as teachers at Lincoln High than he and Glen? Emily had been vice principal and Alice head of the English department. Sure, Alice changed schools on relocation to Ridgewood and lost touch with her former Lincoln High colleagues. A few were invited to her retirement party; none attended. How could they after what had happened?

Yet here they were again, happenstance. Glen talked of Emily's attack after her women's book club. A brutal assault matching Alice's. An iron bar the weapon, said the police officer.

Interrupting his own narrative, Glen looked to Roger. "I'm truly sorry to hear about Alice." He paused, then repeating, "I'm so sorry."

Did Glen believe him? wondered Roger as he walked to the window, lifting a framed photo of a happy family portrait. Glen and Emily seated, their teenage son Brett stood behind. A beautiful family, Glen by far the best looking. The families called him the movie star parent, only better looking than any heartthrob.

"When was this taken?"

"A month before Emily's mugging. We had it professionally done for our Christmas card photo."

"Brett's a lot bigger."

"He's been hitting the weights pretty hard. Over six foot and two hundred pounds. All muscle. He's the team's starting wide receiver."

Roger nodded. "Ken's at six one, two-twenty, with legs like pylons. Plays offense tackle."

"And Katy's attending Ridgewood High?"

"A freshman, can you believe it? Cheerleading, which is what her mother wanted."

Roger replaced the photo, walked by Glen and placed his hand on his shoulder. "Emily was a good person."

Glen's neck tilted like a dog not understanding a command. "She still is. She'll recover."

Different people take different amounts of time. Roger walked away but stopped on hearing Glen. "And wasn't that awful about Bob Reinhardt?"

"Bob Reinhardt? Wasn't his daughter the homecoming queen a few years back? What about him?"

"Didn't you hear? No, I guess you wouldn't. After the incident—" Glen stopped himself. Too close to the unmentionable. He looked at the walls for an escape route. "Bob moved into a one-bedroom Fort Lee condo when his daughter moved out for college. We kept in touch through the hunting lodge. Bob was on the annual Canadian deer hunt when he was shot—" Roger's audible exhale stopped Glen, who waited a few seconds. "I stopped going. Too expensive, saving for... er—" The resurfacing past interrupted. "Just awful what happened to Bob."

"Accident?"

"That's what the report says, but suspicious nonetheless."

Roger's eyebrows dipped.

"Bob's head blown clean off. The bullet exploded on impact. Not deer ammunition, maybe rhino or elephant, I suppose. They never located the hunter who shot him. Identification impossible, would have taken the Canadian Mounties a long time, except the lodge group knew Bob went down that trail alone and was missing."

Glen stopped, while Emily's machines whirred unabated. Roger looked to the sill with its lineup of photos. "Well, I've got to go. Again, I'm so sorry for...?"

Roger felt tapping on his shoulder as he went out the door. Glen held the chocolate box and gift certificate. "You forgot these."

The number three swirled around Roger's head as he sat in his car, engine off. Three people at the same high school. Three attacked. Three sounded like a trend, a pattern. Was it? Why? He needed independent advice. The incident was too delicate to discuss his concern with just anyone. He needed someone outside of northern New Jersey.

Chapter 2

"Dan, you in there?"

The cubicle curtain slid open enough for Roger to recognize the *GQ* drop-dead gorgeous face peering out, knowing Dan was too shy to expose his naked torso concealed behind the curtain.

"Oh, Roger. Hi. Give me a second to finish." The curtain closed with the sound of a wet bathing suit flopping to the floor.

The bright overhead spotlights gave Dan Livorno star quality as he flung the curtain open, now fully clothed. Dan preferred the private cubicle shunned by most UltraFit Health Club members. "Almost finished," Dan said as he fastened the top button of his white shirt.

"You've kept up training." Roger's hand unconsciously touching the last notch of his own thirty-eight-inch belt. "Still fit and trim, I see."

"Mostly swimming and some weights, but nothing like before with Ben." Dan smoothed his shirt. "The service was beautiful."

"Thanks."

"How are you? The kids?"

"We're managing. Ken's into his football. Katy's at the awkward pre-teen age, so she was already moody before... her friends and my sister-in-law have been great helping out though. But, well... you know."

Without responding, Dan lifted his gym bag.

"I should have called, but I thought in person was better than over the phone. I counted on you keeping your early morning routine. Have a few minutes to talk?"

Dan looked at the clock wall. Seven-thirty, making him fifteen minutes behind schedule. Ginny would be home waiting. Dan spoke into his cell without hiding the conversation. He explained to Ginny the circumstance and asked her to dress the children and prepare breakfast for them. He promised to be back in time to take them to daycare and pre-school and ended by telling her he loved her. He turned to Roger. "No problem. Let's go to the juice bar."

They walked past rows of lockers, divining in each row a neighborhood subculture by deodorant and banter: Bergamot and Wimbledon; Lavender and Yankees; Cedar and San Diego Conference. Dan's gym bag swung like a ship's rudder keeping him on course. He never diverted to spy at the bellowing older men strutting naked, their bellies cascading over stubby penises. He avoided eye contact with the two preening narcissists in a row reserved for washboard abs, taut walnut-splitting asses, and glistening V-shaped flying lats. Dan could have joined them if he ever came out from the curtained cubicle. They would have welcomed his magazine-cover good looks for the prestige he would bring. But only Ginny saw Dan naked; not counting the times with Ben, which Dan didn't.

Ben Hausen, UltraFit's owner and a pro-bodybuilder, had matched Dan and Roger for two reasons. First, both sought racquetball partners. Although Dan was fifteen years younger, fitter, and with greater agility than the heavier mid-forties Roger, the former Princeton football player could still summon his athleticism to challenge Dan. With luck, and after the occasions that Dan enjoyed long, special nights with Ginny, Roger even won a few sets.

Ben's other reason was their professional overlap. Dan's one-man company provided theoretical forecast models to financial institutions. Roger managed mega-million trust funds including Ben's in a financial firm of two hundred analysts.

"What's up?" Dan sipped at his protein drink, a remnant from Ben's training.

Roger poured cream into his coffee. "It's hard to explain," he said, then rambled for twenty minutes about his hospital visit, his former neighbor, wives, comas, and brutal attacks. By the time Roger finished air dribbled from his lips, each inhale like sipping through a straw.

"Hearing myself say it out loud... well, it sounds dumb. I guess the surprise at seeing Glen caused my grief to return. I didn't know what to say. I couldn't tell him he would soon be raising his kid on his own like me, could I?"

Dan's eyes blinked; one hand wrapped around his drink, the other rubbed his thigh. He waited, watching Roger's mouth open, a slight jaw movement, expecting that his words might crawl off his tongue rather than being spoken coherently. He heard the faltering description of a man's head blown off. Dan didn't follow the details about the dead man's daughter being a former homecoming queen at the same high school as the battered wives. Roger's pace quickened. Air rushed out of his mouth and was sucked back in the next breath. Dan touched Roger's arm to stop him hyperventilating.

After pausing, Roger said, "I'm rambling. The gun shooting is not the same, but it adds up to three people with violent deaths connected to the same school. It got me thinking." Roger stared into his coffee cup. "If they were stocks, I would say there's correlation without causation. But this feels more like... something. Maybe because it involves my Alice."

With his head tilting forward, Dan's hand covered his left eye like a pirate's patch, elbow on the table. "I'd like to introduce you to my friend Vinnie Briggs, who's also Ben's spouse."

"I know of Vinnie. Not personally but Ben's talked about him during his portfolio planning. Why?"

"He's a detective. Started Briggs Investigative Group, BIG for short." Dan gave a low laugh, not knowing if Roger caught the irony of Vinnie being married to a bodybuilder and calling his agency BIG. "Vinnie's a novice, but with good instincts for human behavior and..." Dan smiled. He had never described Vinnie's private eye career. He trusted his friend's instincts. He explained that years ago Vinnie had applied his innate talent, also called Brooklyn cynicism, to prove embezzlement at Del Vecchio & Neale financial services, their former employer. Dan went on to say that Vinnie's PI skills had continued to improve, if for no other reason than his courses in criminal psychology at John Jay College of Criminal Justice. He qualified for a New York State private investigator certificate, making him legit. Dan heard Roger's approval.

"Good. I'll set it up."

"You don't think I'm reading too much into this?" Roger pushed his coffee mug from the table edge.

"Let's see what Vinnie thinks." Dan's hand returned to rubbing his thigh as he sipped his drink.

***

"Let me get this straight. Your racquetball partner—the guy whose wife's funeral you and Ben attended and who happens to be Ben's financial advisor—he tells you a story. And this guy—"

"Roger."

Vinnie's eyes rolled at Dan's interruption. "Okay, Roger has a hunch his wife's death and the mugging of her colleague who she had not seen in two years are connected. That's the gist?"

Dan smiled. "And the man with his head blown off."

"What?"

Dan smiled wider. "Not relevant, just teasing you." Dan admitted he had thrown in the hunter's death for dramatic effect, knowing Vinnie liked Broadway shows. He laughed out loud at the in-joke, while Vinnie's middle finger whipped out. "Ha ha ha. Come on. Will you talk to Roger?"

Vinnie spread his lips, his smile wider than Dan's. "So now you're fuckin' pimping clients?"

The smile left Dan's face. "Not if you put it like that."

"Oh, sorry, fudgin' pimping clients. Better?"

"Much." Dan laughed, with Vinnie joining in; another in-joke. "Ben told me your cases were becoming too routine and boring." Dan's index finger tapped Vinnie's desk. "Why not spice up your work a little? If I recall, you like spice." Dan chuckled.

"Bullshit. You have a theory so cut the crap. A convoluted math model's clicking in your head. Right?"

"My calculation is that you should diversify your client base or you'll go nuts. Or out of business. Lucky you have a growing stock portfolio." Dan held both hands up, palms outward as if being robbed. "No need to thank me. Just part of my full service." Dan meant his management of Vinnie's large settlement from their past employer, DV&N.

"Full service BS, that's what you provide. And Ben should stop running his fuckin' mouth off every time he sees you."

Dan stood, tapped Vinnie's desk a few times with a grin too wide to fit his face. "Language, Vinnie, language."

"Fudgin', fudgin', fudgin'. Fudgin' happy?"

Dan left Vinnie's office door open as he walked into the outer administrative area to hand Blanca a business card. "Make an appointment for Vinnie to meet this guy."

"Hey, I'm no *puta* slave that anybody can order around." Blanca Santos was the office manager, soothsayer, and peacemaker; she also peppered her language with Puerto Rican curses, which didn't offend Dan as he understood few. Like Vinnie, she had been with Dan at Del Vecchio & Neale during the troubled days.

A voice boomed from the inner office. "Blanca, just make the fu... fudgin' appointment or we'll have him here all day wasting our time."

Blanca swiveled her desk chair to face Vinnie's open office door, her volume matching Vinnie's. "What goes for him goes for you too. Pair of privileged white boys." Blanca swung back holding the business card. She began dialing as Dan leaned over her. "What you standing around for? Move your *blanco culo* now. Can't you see I have calls to make?"

Dan bounced out of the office, happy that his son and daughter had the best godparents ever, constant bickering and cursing aside.

Chapter 3

Vinnie's cursory examination of his fingers showed nothing broken on release of the handshake, which was followed by a perfunctory smile. He pointed with his intact index finger to a single chair in front of the desk while assessing Roger Bryant: big, not Ben-big but taller. He appraised Roger's bigness centered on his midsection, handshake, and ego.

Vinnie slipped into his swivel desk chair. Papers shuffled as he cleared a surface for the computer keyboard.

The usual BIG protocol was to meet clients at their office. Recommendations created the client pool, the first from gays but that soon moved to 'non-denominational.' All cases the same humdrum variations: corporate espionage, employee theft, or an unfaithful spouse, the latter the most boring. Would this be any different?

"First, Mr. Bryant, let me say I'm sorry for your loss," said Vinnie, his voice flat.

"Thanks. As Ben's portfolio manager I feel I know you, so make it Roger. Can I call you Vinnie?"

"Sure."

"I appreciate your taking the time to talk to me. Do you know why I'm here?"

"Dan gave me the gist, but I'd like to hear it from you. Tell me why you think there's a connection between your wife's murder, and the mugging of..." He scanned his computer screen, "...Emily Dingle."

"Dead."

"Excuse me?"

"Emily Dingle died a few days ago."

A brief silence as Vinnie typed on the keyboard, then readjusted his seat to lean back. Everything had just changed. He listened to a precise narrative with a textbook succinct but colorless quality that reminded him of Dan's storytelling. *Are all financial people so mechanical?* Vinnie's eyelids were at half-mast, envisioning the two women's muggings. He often shut his eyes as a client described a case. He alternated between victim's and criminal's viewpoints. He also played games. For corporate crime, he imagined how his thieving father and brother would have done it, supplementing with days at DV&N, the New York financial powerhouse. Mugging, however, came from direct experience, making him thankful for Roger's cursory review.

"I know, sounds crazy to connect them, right?" Roger's eyes fixed on the back of the computer.

"No, it's not." Vinnie's eyes drifted to Roger's midsection. "Uh... you have a gut feeling—" His lips curled. "I mean... in my view... I'll uncover some facts for you to digest." He placed a hand over his face to cover his smile.

After Roger left Blanca stood in front of his desk. "A twenty-five-grand retainer," she said as she fingered the check, holding it to the light. "*Gracias a dios*. Our biggest onetime retainer ever. Vinnie, this is great. I'm going to deposit this now. See you later." Her words were music to Vinnie.

***

Ben's words that night were not music to Vinnie. "Muggings and possible murders. I thought you were done with dangerous shit." Ben stood centered in the condo living room, arms folded, veins popped, and sixty-eight-inch chest inflated.

"It's preliminary and mostly online research to know the people involved—their families, friends, colleagues. Routine shit, not 'dangerous shit' as you put it." Vinnie stood opposite, folding his arms to mirror Ben's stance.

Ben moved to the sofa, his large hands over his face muffling his words. "Again. All over again."

"What's all over again?" It was a rhetorical question and both men knew it. Both knew the answer.

Ben uncovered his face, sputtering his words. "Dan had no right to ask you!"

"He had every right. He's my best friend, aside from you."

Ben looked up, lips pouting. "You're my spouse, so that's kind of implied."

Ben continued to pout, arms twitching as Vinnie continued.

"And you told Dan that I'm bored with the corporate piddle. Bullshit missing documents, laptops lost in transit, former employees using proprietary information. All about money, profit, and protectionism. Boring."

The argument swallowed them, entering the philosophical realm—moral transgressions versus criminal acts. Eventually futile abstraction moved back to the concrete. "And all the infidelity bullshit cases. Being unfaithful is not a crime. Who cares?" griped Vinnie.

"The spouses, partners, boyfriends care. Me, if you cheated, and I know for damn sure you would too if it were me cheating."

This is pointless, thought Ben. He shifted to corporate language, speaking as the owner of a successful business practice. Vinnie groaned, "Same old, same old." Ben continued, repeating that he changed UltraFit Gym to UltraFit Health Club to focus on Manhattan's Upper West Side pool of potential clients. BIG would grow with a reputation in a specialty; it already had a short *New York Times* piece praising BIG's role in uncovering the financial mishandling in a bank's credit division. "Finance is BIG's specialty. You can drop the infidelity cases if you think they're unimportant or boring."

"The *Times* piece was Dan's influence."

"Doesn't matter. You have the start of a specialty reputation. Build on it."

Vinnie stomped, stopped, spread his legs, folded his arms. "You don't get it, do you? I'm bored, and you even said so to Dan. He *gets* it. I need exciting cases, which means I need to expand. We're called BIG—the clue's in the damn name."

A smile shot across Ben's face as he ran to Vinnie, hugged and kissed him by thrusting his tongue into his mouth.

Pushing back, Vinnie gasped, "What... I mean great, but...?"

"Expand. That's it."

"I meant my agency, not my dick."

"How about both?"

"What are you talking about?"

"Rita."

"Who?" Vinnie stepped back. "Wait, you don't mean Barbarella? The Norse beast Valkyrie, ball-crunching man-slayer with armored tits? *That* Rita?"

"Rita Light is a good person. More important, she has martial arts training, is a former women's bodybuilder title holder, and the current reigning Miss Fitness."

"And your point?"

"Hire Rita as your co-investigator. She'll protect you and I know Rita needs the money. She's looking for ways to supplement her income from her UltraFit tae kwon do and karate classes."

"You think I'd work with Barbarella? She knows nothing about being a PI. I can defend myself. I'm strong too."

Ben's right-hand index finger touched his left hand's thumb.

"First, like you said, you need to expand." The right finger moved to the outstretched left's index. "Second, Rita provides security if a situation arises—" Vinnie interrupted, but Ben waved him down. "You're nothing like Rita, and you lack her martial arts training."

Ben's index finger skipped one to touch his ring finger, with Vinnie's wedding ring encircling it. "Third, hiring Rita pleases me. When I'm happy, well..." Ben's hand moved to touch his crotch.

"Sex. You're bribing me with sex."

"It's worked before." Ben loosened his sweatpants and put his hand inside, his gesture a crotch massage.

"Really! Not this time." Vinnie's sour face had a small lifting of his lips; a mere fraction, but not enough to call a smile.

Ben dropped his sweatpants to the floor, revealing his lack of underwear. He flung his sweatshirt to one side. A full-blown Mt. Everest with an erection. With a single flexed arm, a new mountain range emerged. Rushing to Ben, Vinnie kissed him hard, too impatient to wait to be lifted.

Throughout high school and college, Vinnie fantasized his perfect companion. His mate would have a perfect personality, the physical being secondary. Sensitive, sharing, and devoted came first. Maybe a modicum of handsome, and not grossly unfit. Men with bouncing pecs and veiny biceps were a turn-off.

His few romantic liaisons had dissolved as hastily as they had formed. He failed to meet his own criteria. Each ex-partner reeked of insensitivity, self-centeredness, and possessiveness, although all had been reasonably good-looking. Ben satisfied the personality criteria as if he had studied for a 'Vinnie exam.' Ben's failure was the physical. He looked like a cement truck wearing a helmet, sported a haircut better suited to a camel, and a nose that needed GPS guidance to navigate his face. Ben wasn't scary-ugly, just scary.

Yet they married and now Vinnie rushed to his partner, their flesh, sweat, and emotion mashed together.

"I love you. You're my entire world," said Ben, his hot breath tickling Vinnie's earlobe. "I don't know what I'd do if anything..."

"Fuckin' ruin the moment, why don't you?" The words were too hard, but were ameliorated by a kiss. "I love you too. And I worry about you, that's all."

"Me? Why?"

"The heart thing. You know, steroids, hormone and diet pills. Organ failure, comma. Death."

"I see a doctor regularly." Ben stopped. "Nice change of focus, by the way."

Vinnie's grin twisted, his eyelids closing.

"So? Will you?" Ben's voice shifted to office manager again as he climbed off Vinnie.

"Why not? One condition. We fuck on days Barbarella's at the office."

"Her name's Rita and a word of advice—never call her that. She can be gruff, but she'll grow on you."

"Yeah, yeah, like a yeast infection."

"Shut up. Just have patience and listen to Rita. She's smart. College-smart like you. Bet you didn't know that."

"Great. Barbarella can read books."

"Vinnie..."

"Aw, okay, I'll talk to Barba—" Ben jabbed Vinnie's arm.

"Ouch." Vinnie rubbed his shoulder. "Rita."

"Great. I'll set it up." Ben stood up, shaking his ass as he walked across the room. With the distance growing, Vinnie promised to play nice with Barbarella and rushed once more into Ben's arms.

Chapter 4

Vinnie sat at his desk with his furious pumpkin-carved face, glistening green eyes, and voice volume just shy of jet engine, throwing a verbal barrage at Rita.

"Fuck you," said Rita as loudly as Vinnie. "Don't fucking micromanage me!"

"I took the fuckin' PI courses. You've got shit." Vinnie stood behind his desk counterpoised to Rita's side-stretching in the middle of the room as she spoke.

Blanca poked her head into the room. "Everything okay in here guys?"

"Yeah, fuckin' peachy. Routine employee review."

"Sounds like it. I'm getting complaints from Brooklyn." Blanca turned to Rita. "Look, he's a *pendejo* but in his heart Vinnie's not so bad." Blanca stopped. "No, he's a *good* person."

"So you say," sneered Rita.

Vinnie stormed out of the room. A half-hour later he walked in carrying a tray with three lattes and found the women side by side on Blanca's office couch. In the opposite corner he caught sight of Ben leaning on Blanca's desk and the Clydesdale horseshoe triceps in full extension. His workout shirt was soaked and his sweatpants bunched around his crotch. *Oh, shit*, thought Vinnie, who handed Rita a coffee then leaned over to whisper to Blanca. "You fuckin' called Ben?"

Blanca responded so the entire room could hear. "When you... the two of you acted like children, yeah, I called Ben. It was his idea to come here. If I'm forced to play mama, then big *papi* needs to be here too."

On cue, Ben leaned forward. Guitar string sinews twitched accompanied by his masculine bass voice. "This stops now." Steel cables outlined Ben's neck. "I asked you to work together. A favor to you both." Ben's head swung like a construction crane from Vinnie to Rita. "Get over yourselves. Act like adults." Ben's exit was a furious jet stream as he strode out of the office.

"What's with him?" grumbled Vinnie, thumb pointing to the door.

Blanca paused her sipping. "Want big daddy back?"

After mumbling curses, Vinnie said, "Nah, we'll start over." He held his cup with two hands.

Rita raised the coffee with milk to her lips again, nose crinkling, lips protruding. She complained about the effects of too much caffeine until Blanca's long fingernail scraped her arm. Rita's puckered lips blew across the hot liquid. "Yummy."

"Good, we're all clear."

Vinnie recognized Blanca's admonishing pitch, used on her three children. Rita and Vinnie said yes and Blanca left them to discuss strategy.

After ten minutes, Rita came out slamming Vinnie' office door. A minute later Vinnie followed, slamming the door and then the main BIG office door.

***

Vinnie stood over Ben who was prone on the bench, weights strung like fifty-pound blackbirds on a high wire on each side of a barbell suspended above him. A spotter stood behind Ben, a man so large that one of his legs dwarfed Vinnie.

"Listen up," said Vinnie, pressing his finger into Ben's pectorals with no visible indentation. Ben grunted, pushing, face red, arms quivering. With fingers rested underneath the bar, the spotter shouted, "Don't stop. You can do it."

Vinnie ignored the talking mammoth. "Barbarella's a bitch. She'll damage my reputation." Poke, poke.

The barbell tilted. The spotter took hold, guiding the bar to its resting posts. Ben sat up, waiving the spotter away. He stood, grabbed Vinnie's arm, and dragged him across the room as if he was a small child. A few Goliaths gave Ben fleeting glances as he hauled Vinnie behind him, but quickly refocused on the dead-steel graveyard, with getting bigger than Yankee Stadium their main concern. Their dedication to weights was the reason they had privileged access to UltraFit's basement X-room—a windowless subterranean enclave within UltraFit, that needed a separate membership for serious weightlifters and bodybuilders. If you could not lift twice your own body mass you didn't meet the minimum requirement for entry.

Outside the room, Ben's lips filled with spittle as he shouted, "Never interrupt me or anyone during a set. I could have been hurt, or you, or the spotter." Ben's asteroid-size pectorals heaved. With his index finger he poked Vinnie, pushing him into the wall.

Rubbing his chest, Vinnie exhaled the little wind left in his lungs, eyes tearing. Ben grumbled. "We'll finish this at home."

***

Home was a condo penthouse above the UltraFit Health Club. Ben owned the building, providing a family discount to enable the Briggs Investigative Group to rent office space otherwise unaffordable for God.

Vinnie moped, knowing he had made a grave error. *Her fault. She made me do it. Driving me crazy.* He stammered his apology to Ben through three glasses of wine, followed by a convoluted story starting with Dan and ending with Rita.

"Did she listen? Nope, just mouthed her big bravado bullshit. Knows people and more efficient interrogation methods, blah blah et cetera."

Ben listened while consuming Vinnie's three-course apology meal; enough calories for a family of four. Swallowing his last bite, Ben spoke. "Rita's having a rough time. I'll talk to her."

"What rough time?"

"Bad breakup with her boyfriend of ten months. Rita's always had trouble with men."

"Really? I'm shocked."

"Cut the crap, Vinnie." Ben placed his dishes on the kitchen counter then revolved to lean against the sink.

"Here it comes," said Vinnie. "Lecture time."

Rita's story was typical up to a point. Men were drawn to her body, like many men drawn to many women, but her allure was muscles and that made her different. She loved bodybuilding, a profession that barely covered her food bill. Her solution was to exploit the opposite sex.

In peak condition, she could carry two normal-sized men, a huge turn-on for those with a fetish for female bodybuilders. With admirers worldwide, Rita found her niche. Among her fans were wealthy men, able to fly her to four-star hotel suites and pay one thousand dollars plus expenses for a private muscle show. No sex, just flexing and limited touching. Rita knew the risks, took precautions such as leaving her itinerary with friends, announced herself to hotel staff, and filmed her show with a live stream to the cloud. The filming had an added benefit—she sold a copy to the client as a personal tourist souvenir.

"So she works for her living. Like the rest of us."

"Listen to what I'm saying. These men cared only about her body, not her." Ben paused, eyes narrowed. "So she finally meets a guy interested in her and her him, and for ten months it's going great. Then a few weeks ago he gets bored with the flexing and the posing and dumps her."

Insecurity lurked among big and small; academics and laborers; rich and poor. Vinnie once thought bodybuilders were perverted, their bodies gross. Ben shied away from people who didn't lift weights, didn't have the "disease." Their life goals incompatible, except for love. Their near breakup the ultimate insecurity leading to mutual depression.

Ben droned until Vinnie's yawn drowned out his words. "Enough. Rita needs to get laid, I get it. I'll add it to the BIG employee benefits package."

"Vinnie, sometimes you are a jerk." Ben closed the door of his home office as Vinnie went to his BIG office.

On his return, Vinnie heard Ben calling from the living room. "I spoke to Rita. She accepts that she was upset about her breakup. She'll listen to your guidance."

Vinnie rushed to kiss Ben. "You're the best. I worship your big muscles." Vinnie touched Ben's bicep, cooing and laughing.

"Fuck you."

"Exactly." Vinnie's face couldn't contain his smile.

"Want to know these?" Ben flexed then carried Vinnie to their bedroom.

Ben tossed Vinnie overhead like a rubber ball, and he saddled Ben's shoulders. He knew the routine. Ben supported his spine, he leaned back, and enjoyed Ben swallowing his penis.

On release, Vinnie unmounted. "I'll call Barba... Rita tomorrow. Now fuck me to hold up your end, as it were."

Ben wiggled his massive ass at Vinnie.

***

The strained meeting was at least civil. Blanca noticed Vinnie and Rita's every word and gesture. All seemed okay, but not perfect. Rita accepted her need to know regulations and procedures, take courses, and gain a PI license. The big win was for her to agree to follow Vinnie's lead.

Vinnie acknowledged Rita's degree in psychology and martial arts certification. Blanca emphasized the value of Rita's experience at women's crisis and rape centers. "*Comprende? Capisce?* Get it?"

"Yes, Mom. I'll be a good boy."

"*Culo.* Now let's start over."

Blanca reviewed the client's goal. She also explained Vinnie's no-need-for-a-list-or-plan strategy, her eyes rolling like dice in Vegas. "He's like a *pollo* waiting to lay an egg. He knows it will happen, just not when."

Vinnie cursed. "List? Means, motive, and opportunity, that's your list."

"And what about the client's concern?" Rita read from her notepad. "Find out if the three victims are connected."

Vinnie palmed his hands. "They're connected. Why?" He shrugged. "And two victims. The man doesn't fit. Let's learn about the women. I'll call Dan."

"Dan?" Blanca's head tilted.

"Didn't I tell you? Dan's our consultant." Vinnie's hand formed a loose fist and jerked it up and down. "A spreadsheet case is Dan's ultimate wet dream."

Blanca's frown resembled an upturned soup bowl. She turned to Rita. "What do you think of Dan Livorno?"

"Gorgeous hunk. UltraFit women drool over him."

"And men," added Vinnie. "I think of him while I launch into Ben's—"

Blanca jumped. "Vinnie, don't you know when to self-censor?" She walked to her desk. "Meeting adjourned."

Chapter 5

Dan tapped his pen on his desk, more as a prop than a writing instrument. A moment's meditation while waiting for the Excel spreadsheet to open. Two columns, both blank except for two cell entries. The first, nearly all zeroes column had the label SCHOOL ISSUES. The other near-empty column was headed CHILDREN. The two non-empty cells contained the names Ken Bryant and Brett Dingle. In a separate spreadsheet were listings of teachers and administrators in northern Bergen County high schools culled from directories over the last four years. Among the columns in this spreadsheet were columns headed STATUS (living/deceased), a second column headed CAUSE (natural/suspicious), and a third column REASON for the cause. Of all the teachers listed, only Alice Bryant and Emily Dingle had notations among all three columns. Mugging didn't seem sufficient to describe the brutality of Alice and Emily's murders.

Dan picked up his phone, found the contact, and pressed the button. "Vinnie, I may have something here. You'll need to come over to my office for me to explain."

An hour later Dan opened his condo door to Vinnie and Rita squabbling like an old married couple. "Hi, Rita. Vinnie didn't mention you'd be with him, but I'm glad you came."

Vinnie's eyes rolled. Dan knew he would hear about it from Vinnie later, followed by Blanca's revised version, the true story.

Dan pecked Rita's cheek. Vinnie coughed, a fist covering his mouth, making his words unintelligible. Dan rolled his eyes, then ushered the two investigators into his study.

Huddled over Dan's shoulders, Vinnie and Rita watched the mouse pointer flitter over the spreadsheet that filled the screen. Dan explained the general listing of all teachers and staff over a four-year period in the first column. Next to each he explained the various columns, each with a different heading. His mouse pointed to the rows arranged with teachers that had left the school, the corresponding columns providing reasons, such as retirement, illness, pregnancy, birth, spouse relocation, and death. "See the last column?" Dan used the mouse to highlight the CHILDREN & ISSUES heading. "Only two teachers have marks in these columns." He referred to each one, starting with the first. Vinnie exhaled like a wind tunnel.

Dan continued, not stopping for questions. He showed different spreadsheets, churning more numbers. He produced pie charts, cross-tabulation graphs, and recited statistical words that Vinnie thought were probably not in the dictionary and wouldn't count in Scrabble.

Rita turned to Vinnie, who shrugged. Dan continued. "These are outliers. Alice Bryant and Emily Dingle differ from all others in the last four years' records of Bergen County homicides." Dan's mouse highlighted the column labeled HOMICIDE.

"Well, that explains everything. Our work is done." Vinnie slapped his forehead.

"Cut the dramatics. I'm jumping ahead to give you the overview before I explain the theory."

Vinnie sat back, eyes closed, pretending to snore. Rita twisted her torso then assumed a military parade's at-ease position with hands clasped behind her back, legs spread apart.

Ten minutes into the discussion Dan was expounding Tukey's test for range, the mathematical rule for retention, the controversy over data exclusion using truncation or winsorizing, at which point Vinnie formed a pistol with his hand, extended his index finger, and shot himself in the head. "Pow." Rita stifled a laugh.

"Wiseass." Dan was half-frowning and half-smiling. "Do either of you remember the Woburn, Massachusetts, water contamination case?"

"Dan, get real." Vinnie looked to Rita, who was again twisting her body, this time one arm holding her shoulder. She shook her head to indicate she had no clue.

"You go to the movies, don't you? Ever seen the movie *A Civil Action*? Had John Travolta in the lead role? Remember?"

Rita couldn't remember if she did or didn't see it. Vinnie smiled, saying he not only saw it but also owned the DVD in his extensive film collection. "Good plot but no hot sex." Rita's assertive laugh caused Vinnie to flinch.

"If you had paid attention and spent less time undressing every actor in the movie then you would have noticed the story credits a true case."

"Your point?" Vinnie's tongue hung off his lips.

"Give me a chance. In the real case, a contaminated water supply was detected after a few parents accidentally met at Mass General's Leukemia Ward. The movie focused on the lawyers mishandling the case. The part it left out but was included in the book is that the small numbers of children with leukemia were thought of as statistically insignificant. The kids were outliers. The parents didn't see it that way."

"Exactly," said Rita, who stopped twisting. "Our food and water supply are filled with artificial crap. That's why I go organic on everything and since I am no longer in the competitive bodybuilding field, I have no red meat, and poultry only occasionally, and—"

"We fuckin' get it." Vinnie heard Dan's moan. "We fudgin' get it. No need to hear your diet and grocery list." Vinnie's lemon-sucking scowl matched Rita's puckering lips.

She spread her feet wider. "Diet is important. There's no need to use steroids to have a strong body, not like some people." She glared at Vinnie. "How much did you use to bulk up? Looks like you could use another shot, you're a little... *lacking* in some areas."

Dan jumped up before Vinnie answered. "Look, if you two don't mind can we get back to your case?"

This was not Vinnie. Dan had never heard him this argumentative and disparaging. He didn't know Rita well; they only talked a few times at UltraFit. Ginny's comment after one of Rita's tai chi class had been, "Rigorous and enjoyable." Dan translated this to mean exhausting and relentless. He would call Blanca for an explanation as soon as Vinnie and Rita left, and thought it best not to tell Ben or Ginny.

Tapping his pen, Dan continued, "In the Woburn case, door-to-door data collection by hundreds of volunteers produced an analysis showing that the industrial solvent trichloroethylene contaminated the town's water supply. Mathematicians dismissed the few children as random outliers, but they were not."

Rita stretched her arms and bent down into a squat. "What does this mean for us? Canvass all of Bergen County's school population for dead teachers with children?"

"Not yet," Dan chuckled, with Vinnie and Rita stone-faced. "Start with the two outliers at Lincoln High. If you'll notice, I've marked the boys with footnotes. In my notes I found their school attendance odd. Both sons attended the same high schools as their mothers, although not at the time of their mothers' attacks. You need to find additional connections."

"Like what?" Vinnie was leaning in, his eyes no longer drooping.

Dan moved his mouse to highlight a column headed SCHOOL AWARDS. "See, both received athletic recognition. Now look at my column labeled LEGAL. I noted Alice Bryant and Emily Dingle with question marks."

"Holy fu… fudgin' hell. Maybe it's not them but their kids." Vinnie was smiling.

"Exactly. Look again at my notes. Both Ken and Brett missed being on the high school football team roster in the same year. Is this a connection? Why?"

Vinnie stood up, and leaned over the computer to tap the screen. Dan pushed Vinnie's finger away. "Don't touch, just point or describe. I've told you this many times."

Vinnie patted Dan's shoulder. "Oh, I forgot you're sensitive about your computer. Do you take it to bed with you at night?"

Dan took a cloth and wiped the screen.

With a sigh, Vinnie said, "This means more data to show whether or not the two rows are true outliers or part of a bigger picture."

"Exactly." Dan's chest puffed. He had known from the day he hired Vinnie as his assistant he had a working brain able to perform critical thinking. "We need direct information on Ken and Brett. The town newspaper's school sporting events specifically mentions their absence. They are missing from the Lincoln High Facebook football rosters the year before their mothers' muggings. I'd guess disciplinary action but juveniles are never listed in the police blotter. You'll need to learn more about them."

Rita walked closer to Dan. "And you think they'll just tell us, no problem?"

Dan smiled as he looked up to Rita stretching, her 1960 Cadillac ass and tits. Dan turned to Vinnie, ignoring Rita; every night he saw more curves than the Amalfi coast in bed with Ginny. "Yes, if you follow Vinnie's lead. He's good at this."

Vinnie's grin extended across his face, almost hitting the walls. "One more question. I don't see Bob Reinhardt's name anywhere."

"That's right. He wasn't affiliated directly with the school. His only connection was his daughter. He was shot in Canada and the Canadian authorities declared it a hunting accident, although they were unable to explain the rhino ammunition. They assumed they were illegally using prohibited rounds."

"But isn't he also an outlier?"

"No. He's an anomaly."

Vinnie shook his head, hair flopping, arms thrown overhead. "Math mumbo jumbo."

"Nope. If we listed everyone associated with the school such as parents, grandparents, cousins we would have no end. Even if we limited it to parents, the list that were attacked or died over four years would include car accidents, cancer patients, heart attacks, disease, and domestic violence. A long list of anomalies. I've started with strong connections, teachers and staff, because that's what your client Roger Bryant suspects."

"Like I said, math mumbo jumbo." Vinnie walked out, closing the front door behind him, leaving Rita with Dan.

Chapter 6

Vinnie entered the code to the electronic lock on the gold-leaf-etched door.

Briggs Investigative Group (BIG)
Vincent Briggs, PI

He held the door for Blanca while summarizing events at Dan's condo. He was thankful Blanca didn't scream in the hallway. Screaming made her feel good; him, not so much.

"I felt bad. We were getting along so well, but I don't want her on interviews. I don't like her style, and the fuckin' twisting drives me crazy. You should have heard the mouth on her. A masochist having a bad day."

"Listen up, *niño*, Rita needs to learn how to conduct interviews. Besides, the girl might talk more to Rita. As for her brother, Rita's big boobs will make him think with his little dick unless he's gay. And if he is gay then you take over." Blanca laughed.

Slurping coffee, Vinnie said, "We have one shot. She better not screw it up. And she has to stop the fuckin' twisting and stretching... it's nuts."

The front door swung open as Blanca stowed her high-heel shoes under the desk. Vinnie froze seeing Rita. Blanca chirped out, "Good morning, Rita. Early, isn't it? You want herbal tea?" Blanca's smile lingered a few seconds.

"It's okay." Rita held up a water bottle. "I've come from my morning class. Get an early start." Rita looked to Vinnie, who walked away. She twisted. "Actually, there's another reason. I had a sleepless night. I owe you an apology." She moved to Vinnie, who stepped backward, bumping into Blanca's desk.

"I've been a real bitch—one hundred percent crazy. My breakup has, I don't know, been hard. It doesn't excuse my actions."

"I get it. You need a good fu—"

Blanca's cough sounded like a cannon. "And, Vinnie? You have anything to say?"

Chewing his tongue, Vinnie said, "I guess I've been an asshole too. This case is important for the agency. Unknown territory for us, going to Jersey and all."

The women laughed.

"What's so fuckin' funny?" Vinnie's frown gave way to a strained smile.

They assembled in Vinnie's office. Blanca reviewed the interview requirements of the deceased women's children. "Remember," she advised, "they are grieving but teenagers don't show it like adults."

"Okay," said Vinnie. "Blanca will set up appointments this week." Vinnie paused. "We're going to fuckin' Jersey." As the women laughed again, Vinnie's hiccupped snicker gave weak solidarity.

Rita hated to mention it, but she had a conflict. A prior commitment to judge an out-of-town women's fitness contest the entire week. She could back out, lose the pay, but she would have to forget future judging gigs.

While not exactly smiling, Vinnie's teeth showed. "No problem if—"

Blanca clapped her hands to interrupt. "You can work using the hotel's Internet to collect online school announcements and newspaper articles. Report by email or Skype. Upload reports and sensitive matters to the BIG cloud account. I'll set up your password."

Rita asked Vinnie to clarify the types of material needed. Vinnie pointed his index finger at Rita. "Good question. This is how we work together."

Blanca told Vinnie to stop the pontification and spit it out.

"That's not what I call office spirit." His face contorted.

"You're being childish and an asshole."

Vinnie strutted. "Casting a wide net helps when facts are vague, especially to uncover motive."

Blanca took Rita's arm and walked her out. "*Un hombre* who walks like his balls are too big for his pants."

Vinnie returned to his swivel chair, clasping hands behind his neck. He imagined Ben's satisfaction upon learning he had insisted Rita not cancel her judging contract. *Magnanimous of me when you think about it.* Vinnie adjusted his crotch, thinking of Ben's appreciation.

***

Crossing the upper deck of the GW Bridge, Vinnie's head turned to glimpse one last Manhattan skyline view. He entered the Village of Ridgewood, pedestrians oozing out of upscale shops to return to their landscaped homes manicured by immigrant labor and kept in manure by Wall Street money.

He stood outside a two-story stone building. *Just your average seven-bathroom home.* Somewhere from within a dog barked.

"Lester, quiet." Roger Bryant held a chocolate Labrador's collar as he opened the front door. "I was on a call. Come in."

Vinnie shook Roger's hand, apologizing for his colleague Rita Light's absence due to a previous out-of-town commitment. The Labrador's nose nudged Vinnie's backside.

"Go to the kitchen!" commanded Roger.

Vinnie followed the dog until he felt a tug. "Not you."

In the large family room, a teenager sprawled on the couch, eyes riveted to a seventy-inch wall-mounted TV. Two hands clutched a remote control moving a cartoon soldier away from a band of assassins.

"Ken, this is Mr. Briggs. He's here to help investigate mom's..."

The teenager's head turned, eyes sunken, lips flicking. "Hi ya." An explosion boomed through the surround sound speakers. "Ah, shit."

"Vinnie, my son Ken, who had better watch his language. My daughter Katy is at a friend's house but she's due back anytime soon. Ken would be at football practice but this is exam week. As you can see, he's studying."

Vinnie estimated Ken to be over six feet by one or two inches with arms and shoulders suggesting more time lifting weights than books.

"Let's go to my study first."

Roger pointed Vinnie to a black leather high-back chair facing a window. "Scotch or beer?"

"I'm fine." Vinnie glanced at his watch as Roger sat with his Scotch: it was just past ten-thirty.

Vinnie asked permission to record his interview, especially with the children. "A recording preserves details I might forget," he explained. After pulling a small recorder from his briefcase he pushed it aside, without retrieving his notepad and roadmap of questions; he hoped this showed that the talk was a simple get-to-know-the Bryant-family exchange.

Roger's review of the basics proved Vinnie's surmise was correct: the Bryant family were among the privileged one percent upper-middle class. Alice Bryant had been a high school English teacher before entering administration. After the move to Ridgewood she changed schools, sick of the winter commute to Lincoln High. She found she didn't fit the new school's ethos so took early retirement at the age of fifty.

Vinnie stifled a yawn. "And how are Ken and Katy?"

"Much as you'd expect. Ken hangs out with his football teammates. He's quiet, but he never said much before... Typical secretive teenage boy. I'm sure he surfs porn, drinks beer, smokes pot, but I don't think he's into any hard drugs. Well, maybe steroids," said Roger with a snicker. "I'm kidding. I hope not. But, I mean look at him. Nearly two hundred twenty—I didn't reach that until Princeton, and I'm two inches taller."

"What happens when he graduates next year?"

"He'll play in college. Not Big Ten but Division One or Mid-Atlantic. Full athletic scholarship, not that we need it. Football will gain him entry, which is why grades don't concern him as long as he graduates. His mother worries... worried. Wanted him to do well academically. The school teacher in her. She's proud of him... was. Me too."

"For his football ability?"

"Yes. And because he's a buff, good-looking guy. I supply him with condoms. He used a box in three months but he's sharing with teammates. Imagine him among horny college girls? To be young again." Roger clicked his tongue. "You sure about that beer or Scotch?"

"Thanks, just a few minutes with Ken alone."

"I'll be in my study." Roger picked up the TV remote and turned the television off.

"Hey, I was in the middle of—"

"Middle of nothing. You'll talk to Mr. Briggs and turn off the goddam video game."

Vinnie waited until Roger left the room. "I'm sorry about your mother."

"It's what happens in life, isn't it?"

"No, it's not. Your mother's murder is not what happens."

"Yeah."

"Tell me what you remember. Any idea why your mother was attacked?"

"How the fuck should I know?" Spoken with a teenager's charm.

Vinnie raised his eyebrows.

"What?" Ken was fidgeting with a throw pillow.

"Tell me about football. Is a football career what you plan after college?"

"Probably. Offensive tackle." Ken flexed his arm, which Vinnie knew was half Ben's and not nearly as cut, yet still impressive for a teenager. *Just my luck, Ken's the one-in-a-hundred atypical adolescent who is neither introverted nor reticent among strangers. Arrogant prick.*

"What will you study in college?"

Ken shrugged.

"If football doesn't work out, would you become a high school teacher like your mother?"

His laugh was a bark as if from the Labrador sprawled on the rug.

"What's funny?" Vinnie looked to the dog for an explanation.

"High school. Idiots, little wimps. Me and my teammates could take on the entire school, whip their puny asses. I can't imagine being with those losers for the rest of my life."

After ten minutes waiting for Katy, Vinnie entered Roger's office and he made several calls to his daughter with no luck. Roger fumed, so Vinnie said his goodbyes and left.

***

He drove along Route 17 north to Mahwah, circled the modern brick Lincoln High and examined the football stadium and track laid out over two acres. Although it was vacation week, the full faculty parking lot suggested a teachers' meeting, except he was puzzled by a florist's and catering van at the front entrance. An out-of-term celebration?

Vinnie continued to the New York State border and crossed the Hudson via the Tappan Zee Bridge. It was an easy drive along Old Saw Mill Parkway to Manhattan until an accident on the Henry Hudson Parkway stopped traffic, giving Vinnie time to speak to Blanca using his hands-free cell.

He failed to see the need to return to Ridgewood to interview Katy Bryant as Blanca suggested. "Why? And bring Rita? Waste of time." Vinnie inched along with the stop-go traffic, like his summary of the interview. The Bryants were self-centered elitists with no connection to anyone but themselves. He suggested they focus on the Dingle son. Blanca agreed but did not relent on Katy Bryant.

Chapter 7

"Yeah, whatever," said Katy Bryant to Vinnie when he asked permission to record her.

They were in the family room where Vinnie first met Katy's brother. Blanca pointed out that without interviewing the Bryants' daughter the investigation was half-assed, and Rita needed to talk to Ken too. Vinnie protested, which expanded his knowledge of Spanish curses, and Blanca practiced throwing her pen.

Lester, the ass-sniffing Labrador, lay next to Vinnie, who thought either the dog approved of his smell or distrusted him. Smart dog, either way. The interview began with Katy; this time it was Ken's turn to be a no-show. Katy said something about her brother's football practice and he would be home in a half-hour. Vinnie didn't really care if Ken showed up, steadfast that interviewing him twice was a waste of time.

Katy sat cross-legged, touching her toes, as if they were newly discovered. She acknowledged Vinnie and Rita's condolences with a grunt. Vinnie began asking a series of small-talk questions about Mrs. Bryant, receiving Katy's revolving responses of "Good," "Nice," "Drove me," "Guess so," "Dunno," "A regular mom," "You know." The latter being the most frequent reply.

Vinnie reclined, sinking into the sofa. With a half-turn he gestured for Rita to try. Scratching her nose emphasized her masculine-sized arms. She insisted on dressing in tight Lycra workout clothing to emphasize her bust. Her pants outlined strong thighs and a tight butt. She chose the outfit for Ken's benefit, if he showed up.

Rita looked around the room. "Beautiful potted plant." She walked to the windowsill, which was wide enough to sit five people. "I've never seen an indoor cyclamen this large." She took hold of the tag, which said Fine Flowers. "I must remember this place. Your father's choice or your mother's?"

"They were at the funeral home for me when I got there. Weird. Our maid takes care of them."

Rita returned to her seat, remembering Katy's reluctance to answer Vinnie's earlier questions. His line of inquiry did not suit an adolescent girl, either too gay or too automaton. Katy refolded her legs under her, and Rita mirrored the position. Vinnie understood the signal and sat back. Rita's voice hushed, as if telling a secret. "I lost my mom when I was a teenager."

"Geez, I didn't know that," said Vinnie a little loud, leaning forward.

With a poke in his side, she moved him back. Rita placed her hands on each thigh, glad that Katy's eyes had remained focused on her feet folded under her.

"It was hard. I missed her so much. She was like a friend to me," Rita continued, counting seconds like cross-training. "Protected me from my conceited older brother. He bugged the hell out of me. Thought he was better than me. And I'm sure my dad favored him during the... the whole thing."

Katy pouted while pulling her toes. "Ain't that the truth."

"Same for you?"

"Yeah, my dad treats my brother like a god just because he plays football and lifts weights."

Rita's offer to train Katy met with derision and an impolite comment about her masculine look. "Last thing I want is big arms like yours. Bad enough I have to watch my brother strutting around flexing and posing."

"Does he only do that in front of you?" asked Vinnie, holding Rita to prevent her stretching one arm behind her neck.

"You wish. He, like, flexes in front of the mirror all the time. In front of kids at school. Looks like a jerk. Says, 'Bet you wish you had guns like these.' He's an asshole. His Facebook password is 'bigbadmotherfucker,' like I couldn't find the Post-it stuck under the lamp on his desk."

Vinnie leaned across, blocking Rita, and said, "What about his friends? Are they like him?"

"Sort of. I mean a couple of guys treat me okay when they come over but most are like my brother and think they rule the world."

Rita pulled Vinnie back now that they had found their tag-team rhythm. "What does your dad think? What did your mom feel about this?"

"Dad just thinks Ken is *numero uno*. Mom went along, even when he got in trouble. She defended him."

"Trouble?" said Vinnie, his voice a hollow pretense of surprise.

"Yeah, at Lincoln, you know, his last school? He beat up a freshman and sent him to hospital with broken bones and stuff."

"Geez, was he arrested?" said Rita who was twisting her torso again.

"Duh, no. Well, he would have been but Mom and Dad got him off on a minor charge. The football coach helped, you know, like talked to the cops that had been on his team as students. They're old guys, like thirty. They sucked up to the coach and Ken got away with it."

"Ken didn't do it?" asked Vinnie.

Katy's sarcastic laugh stopped with her hand covering her mouth. "Oh, he did it. Told me he beat the crap out of a 'little pussy' for telling their algebra teacher that Ken forced him to do his take-home quiz. Like, duh, as if the teacher didn't know. I mean, my stupid brother getting all the right answers on his own? As if."

"What happened?"

"You know, Dad like paid off the kid's parents big-time. He was furious. Mom got the school not to expel him, but he couldn't play on the stupid football team. Permanently banned. We had to move to this fucking place so he could play football again. I lost all my friends because of him, the bastard."

The door opened and in walked Ken carrying his football gear. He looked at his sister, then to Rita and Vinnie. Katy got up and left the room. "Practice ran overtime. Sorry."

Vinnie said it was not a problem, which sounded as sincere as Ken's apology. Rita stood, hand extended, back arched, breasts at full mast, nipples aimed at Ken's chin. Ken shook Rita's hand while his eyes roamed over her boobs.

"Mind if I get a drink? I'm dry from the heavy workout." He walked out rubbing his hand.

Vinnie turned to Rita. "Really? Mangle his hand, why don't you?" Rita made a sucking sound.

Ken returned with shirt unbuttoned showing chest hair, his sleeves rolled to his elbow. He went to the chair vacated by his sister. He basked in Rita's compliment about his physical condition. His return compliment mentioned her "tight, packed body."

Rita twisted again, her fingers tapping her thigh. "What was it like for you at Lincoln with your mother being a teacher there?"

"Nothing great. I'm doing better here. Better team and coaching."

It was Vinnie's turn. "Not what I heard."

Ken sprang up, a small amount of his sports drink spilling onto his chest. "And what did you hear?"

Vinnie smiled. "You know, the suspension. You beating up a freshman."

"That was bullshit."

"So you couldn't take a freshman? I guess you weren't as big as you are now." Rita held back from a full smile.

"More bullshit. I could take down any of those punk-ass freshmen. Look at these guns." Ken rolled up his sleeve to his shoulder and flexed.

"Pretty good, but would they really scare anyone? I mean I'm not scared." Rita's smile widened.

"Fuck you, bitch."

Vinnie had never moved so fast, reaching Rita in time to stop her. He reminded her that she knew meditation and self-control methods.

Rita walked out. Vinnie turned to Ken. "Consider this your lucky day."

"Why?"

"You'll be able to finish your football season."

"Her take me down? Fuck you too."

Vinnie walked out wishing his intervention had been slower.

They rode in silence until they passed the George Washington Bridge tollbooths lined up like soldiers.

"Men think they can beat and abuse women. I could have made sure Kenny-boy doesn't have children." Rita didn't stifle her lingering anger.

"And what good would that do us?"

Rita shrugged.

"Yet we learned something. He's a bully and his sister doesn't like him. His mother probably protected him at Lincoln High, despite his role in a violent altercation. Let's find out what else happened at that school." Vinnie's lips puckered, whistling as they drove along the West Side Highway.

Cause and Excuse

Chapter 8

Nothing. Two hours and nothing. Blanca fumed. She had perused the Lincoln High Facebook page and covered the last three years of posts, activities, and galleries. Typical stories on sports, academic honors, field trips to Paris, Washington, and exchange students from Poland, Scotland, and Germany. Engagements too. "Who marries at eighteen anymore? Don't young people live together these days?" She leaned back rubbing her eyes.

"Ben and I married." Blanca's stare brushed the smirk from Vinnie's face. "And did you check teachers too?"

"Sometimes you're a real pain in the *hinchapelotas*." Blanca tapped her rear end. "And no, I haven't checked on teachers. What have you done?"

Vinnie patted his mouth over a yawn. "I had a rough night."

"I don't want to hear about it."

"Killjoy. Half the fun is in the telling."

"You brag worse than my boys after they win a Little League game. Snot nose. *Tiras el moco.* Go away. I need time to myself."

The reprieve suited Vinnie. He had called several northern New Jersey police departments and each was a time-waster: kept on hold; answered desk officer's same inane questions; transferred to a detective with repeated questions and eventual non-interest.

The last detective summarized the common opinion: "Let me get this straight. Two teachers were attacked and subsequently died. Both were parents and had sons who were students at Lincoln High School. And in one case the woman and her son had moved to Ridgewood. And then, as you said, the 'unrelated but interesting Canadian hunting accident.' I'm sorry, Mr. Briggs, but this is the real world, not a TV cop show. Goodbye."

Hearing his story repeated, Vinnie thought the whole investigation sounded lame. He called Dan to whine his frustration.

"That's the problem with outliers," said Dan. "They don't fit a discernible pattern initially."

This wasn't going Vinnie's way. Maybe telling Dan about his night with Ben would help. Nah, he decided that most heteros didn't get it. Vinnie smiled recalling Dan's brush with gay sex, with Ben no less. Dan didn't agree with Vinnie's view that the upside of that incident proved for sure he wasn't gay. Dan had become red-faced, sputtered that he already knew *for sure*, and told him never to mention it again—ever. *Nope, better not describe his night with Ben.*

During lunch, Blanca walked into Vinnie's office carrying her salad and protein drink, her diet designed by an UltraFit nutritionist. She plopped into a chair placing her food on his desk.

"I'm a lunch counter? Would you like fries with that, ma'am?"

Blanca twirled a piece of lettuce on her fork then shoveled it into her gaping mouth displaying her latest filling. "Here's the thing, I've cross-checked obits and Lincoln High's roster going back four years. Six dead teachers. Two from unspecified health problems, one heart attack, and two from cancer. The last has no cause listed but there was no report of foul play either." Blanca paused, another lettuce leaf and tomato segment pitched into the cavern.

"*Nada*, that's what you're telling me?"

"Almost. While perusing—"

Vinnie laughed. "I hope you're reading the dictionary on your own time. *Perusing*." Blanca was not smiling. Interrupting Blanca pushed one of her hot buttons, but it was such fun.

"Bet your ass you're sorry. Can I continue?" Blanca waited for Vinnie's non-verbal apology with a bow and praying gesture. Her frown disappeared. She pushed buttons too.

"So, like I was saying, I decided to scan all the obits for one time period and I found a teenager's death notice three years back, a former Lincoln High student but not at the time of her death."

"No way."

"Way. Going back to the previous year I found another former Lincoln High girl died, again while attending another school."

"So unrelated to our case." Rubbing his chin, Vinnie swiveled his chair to look out his window. A light snow fell. "Causes, actual or probable?"

Walking around Vinnie's desk, Blanca took her empty Styrofoam lunch box and put it in his wastebasket. She then moved to the window, blocking Vinnie's view. As if matching her words to the falling snow, she whispered, "*Suicidar*," but the Spanish did not alter the past. "No newspaper articles on their deaths, but obits referenced the funeral homes handling the burials with online sympathy listings."

Vinnie stood next to Blanca. Although he wasn't tall, his six inches over the diminutive Blanca enabled him to rest his arm on her shoulder. Blanca continued her monologue. Following the names of a few friends, she had looked at their social media pages. In both suicide cases a few students posted about bullying, citing this as the reason why the two girls left Lincoln High. Blanca paused, as if her words cancelled the facts.

"Guess this means visiting parents, right?"

"You have an appointment tomorrow afternoon with one, another two days later with the other."

Vinnie lowered his forearm. "Would you like to do them?"

Blanca turned from the white snowfall to Vinnie's face, which seemed whiter. "Nice try, *cariño*, but—" Blanca paused, turned back to the window, and said, "Not a snowflake's chance in hell."

***

The mother wept, fingers pulling tissues from a box like plucking grapes off stems. Words slithered from her throat. A sob for each insult slung at her daughter. Tenacious, unstoppable slurs. No amount of pleading with the bully's parents or the bully changed anything. The ringleader had once been their daughter's friend in grade school. Out of nowhere, the former friend was on a crusade to make their daughter an outcast, identify trivial faults, or simply invent pernicious rumors.

Through sniffles and wiping her eyes, the mother continued. Vinnie saw the grief that pivots on anger. The mother's words a cauldron, bitter laughs bubbling at the school's zero-tolerance yet indifferent attitude for the special circumstances. A star athlete, cheerleader, homecoming queen, and wealthy. The dead girl's father scoffed. He knew money or political clout outweighed moral obligation. He wanted to puke on the admin excuses: "We do what we can but we are limited." "Our hands are tied." "It's a free speech issue."

"We were handed the blame-the-victim script," said the mother, eyes blood-red. She recited the litany. "'We suggest your daughter avoids going online and social media.' 'We've advised your daughter not attend athletic events.' 'Maybe your daughter could dress differently, call less attention to herself.' 'Have you considered changing schools?'" The mother paused. "Well, we changed her school and little good that did."

"Our daughter endured three inconsolable years," explained the father while Vinnie's and Rita's eyes grazed the wall photos, like a frame-by-frame movie. The attractive ten-year-old on one wall morphed into a waif in her last photo, a premonition of her premature death shrouded in sadness.

If their first parent interview was harsh, the second was raw. Again Vinnie and Rita examined the picture parade on walls, table tops, and the TV stand. The girl was neither too thin nor overweight. Her purple-streaked short hair did not flatter her plain face, but otherwise she was an average teenage girl. Appearance was not her problem. Her coming out announced in her sophomore year was. "Her problem," said the mother, voice high-pitched, still incredulous that being a lesbian was an issue in today's enlightened era. "This is not the nineteen-fifties." The mother described the taunting her daughter received, labeled 'penis-envy bitch.'

Vinnie cringed. Hearing the garbage words recalled similar insults slung at him. He did not have to contend with a worldwide social network delivery system. Vinnie's chest cavity constricted, his head aching, and he wanted to cover his ears. The grieving mother retreated to her safe refuge, a veil of tears.

***

"I'll upload the details to the BIG account, but I don't need your number-crunching to know there's a link somewhere." Vinnie talked to Dan using the cell speaker as he prepared supper.

"Unlike you, I prefer to crunch numbers to confirm your instinct and determine statistical significance." A cooing followed Dan's words, his daughter approving of Dan's diaper-changing technique.

At the end of the conversation with Dan, Vinnie called Rita. Her first words broadcast a lingering melancholy. Her delayed response was so long Vinnie thought she had hung up. He expected Dan's number-crunching report around nine pm and he would call her immediately after.

With a short cough, Rita said she might not be able to answer at that time as she had an appointment to meet someone.

"Someone you know?" Vinnie didn't care but he had a curiosity habit for gossip honed over many years.

"Not yet."

"So, you're not sure and might be available tonight for an update. I mean—"

Rita replied with a half-suppressed titter. "I know what you mean. And I'm sure. What I seek... um, need, well, after today I'll get what I need. *Do you know what I mean?*"

Silence was Vinnie's answer. The parents' interviews had unnerved them. Who could fail to be upset hearing parents speak of their teenager's depression, bullying, social media taunting, and resulting suicide?

Dan's call finally came around ten o'clock. "Too late?" he asked.

"Nah. I'm doing online research."

"Oh." Dan paused. "Uh... uh... no need to explain. I'll call tomorrow then."

"No, dumbass, not that kind of research." Vinnie chuckled. Dan was so easy to embarrass.

"Sure. Um... your suicides suggest they are neither random nor unrelated. Yes, different years, and transfers from Lincoln. Difficult to make connections. Suicide motive obvious, but not specific. And why no flags by the police? You'll need to go further afield."

"A fuckin' mystery, is that what you're telling me?"

"Not my choice of words, but yes. You have your work cut out. I'm going to bed... to do my own research with Ginny." Dan's pinched laugh brought a hardy bellow from Vinnie. A few years before Dan would not have been able to make the slightest reference to sex, so Vinnie viewed Dan's metaphor as solid progress.

Vinnie sent Rita a text: 'Meet in the morning. Unless you had a hard night.' Vinnie smiled. *Metaphors can be fun*. Rita texted okay with a smiley puckered emoji. Was that for his metaphor or her hard night? Did she text while...? Vinnie swaggered into the bedroom, eyes on Ben upright in the bed. His naked torso wider than the king headboard, head buried in his Kindle. Vinnie knelt at the bed as if saying nighttime prayers. "Want to do some research?"

Chapter 9

The modest single-story brick building for Barnetto and Dingle, LLP, CPA, in the Fair Lawn, New Jersey Office Park, didn't surprise Vinnie. As he anticipated, the building was a boring, small, square, concrete high-rise with a symmetrical vertical facade and a flat roof.

Vinnie arrived early for his appointment, so with nothing better to do he observed traffic from the waiting room window. A white van passed with Fine Flowers printed on the side panel, recalling that Rita had suggested they bring Blanca a large bouquet; that thought and a glance at the empty seat beside him reminded him of Rita's absence from the Dingle interview, this time to judge the San Antonio Women's Fitness Regional Championships. He had complained to Ben about Rita's many commitments. "How many contests can she judge? Why not just one big event?" Dimpled cheeks and upward curled lips mitigated Vinnie's sour complaint to Ben, who had explained it to him many times. More competitions were good for the bodybuilding business and for bodybuilders trying to gain reputations. Vinnie argued that with all the contests it guaranteed everyone a trophy within some inane category. "Sideshows to sell useless products, that's the real reason?" Sarcasm earned Vinnie a toss on the bed for Ben's special sideshow, and Vinnie awarded Ben a trophy.

Vinnie googled the florist van name and saved the telephone number into his address book. A man brushed past to exit. Vinnie watched him enter a waiting black, late-model sedan, probably an Uber. A voice startled him. Standing above Vinnie was a long-legged man, well toned, and with a perfect complexion, suggesting a return from a tanning appointment and a personal training session. An extended arm with open hand neared Vinnie's head.

"Glen Dingle. Sorry for the wait."

Wow. Great voice, super handsome, and buff. The trifecta.

"Vinnie Briggs. Thanks for taking time to meet me." Vinnie repeated to Glen the same reason Blanca had given for the appointment: to investigate Glen's wife's murder and Roger Bryant's. "I'm so sorry for your loss."

"Thanks. It's been very hard. How can I help?"

Vinnie went with Dan's suggestion to emphasize data and statistics. He talked about outliers, probability, and that Glen Dingle and Roger Bryant's wives being teachers at the same school was unusual.

Glen Dingle shrugged.

"I know, a stretch, but could be significant," Vinnie agreed.

"It is not impossible but I'm not convinced," Glen said.

Rather than debate the numbers, Vinnie drifted to Glen's son Brett. He started with concern for the boy's health after his mother's death.

"He's upset, as you'd expect, but he's not asked for special help. Is there such a condition as an undiagnosed depression?" Glen appeared to meditate on his rhetorical question. With a negative head motion, his half-smile brightened on his handsome face. "Football and wrestling occupy his time. I'd like to think team involvement shows he's coping."

"What about the Bryant children? A son and daughter, right?"

"I can't say. They moved away two years ago. Ridgewood. I only knew the daughter by sight. She's younger than the boys. Didn't attend Lincoln. I don't keep up with Ken's sports activity."

Vinnie's chin moved to his chest, mouth closed as he waited.

Glen's lips tightened. "Ken was on the Lincoln High football team before he transferred. I suppose he might still play."

"Aren't their schools in the same league? Do you not go to Brett's games? Maybe see Ken on the field."

With a quick glance at his wristwatch, Glen said, "I have an appointment in a few minutes. Anything else I can help you with?" Glen's chair moved slightly back from the desk.

"I am curious," said Vinnie. "I heard Brett and Ken were buddies. Didn't they stay in touch?"

"I don't see how my son's friendship relates to my wife's murder. Please leave my son out of this. He has nothing useful to add to your investigation." Glen's voice was harsh, the mellow warmth at the start of the interview now entirely absent from his tone.

"I understand. However, all views add new information, new data points. Did anything happen between your son and Ken Bryant?"

Glen stood. "I'm sorry, I have to prepare for my next meeting." His voice was gruff as he held open his office door. Vinnie ambled to take Glen's extended hand, promising to keep him abreast of relevant developments. Glen Dingle's good luck wishes sounded hollow as he closed his door, reminding Vinnie to not involve his son.

***

Rita and Vinnie sat facing Roger Bryant in a corner office on the thirty-seventh floor of a glass and steel building in a prestigious Madison Avenue location. Comparing the office of the man in front of him and that of Glen Dingle was like comparing a major league ballpark to a child's sandbox. Roger Bryant was a high-end earner. Vinnie wished he had asked for more than a twenty-five K retainer.

Blanca made the interview appointment under the guise of the usual BIG progress update to clients.

"I'm afraid we have found little as yet, but we're hoping to be more definitive in a few weeks." Vinnie used his best professional-sounding voice.

"So you don't think there's a connection?"

"The outliers are few. Our investigation on your behalf has little to link your wife's murder to that of Emily Dingle. We're thinking the connection is looser, through common friends or activities such as bowling, a book group, that sort of thing." Vinnie had warned Rita his questions might seem odd, intended to throw Roger off from the real point of the meeting.

What threw Roger off was Rita's crushing handshake. He placed his throbbing hand under the desk and avoided looking at her, focusing on Vinnie instead. Rita surveyed the office.

Behind Roger, framed photos sat on a bookcase. Typical family moments caught on camera. The center photo displayed four people huddled and smiling into the lens, a decorated tree in the background—the Christmas card snap. Another was a professional, gold-framed image of Alice Bryant; background lighting color-balanced her on all sides, flawless complexion and makeup, perfect hair. Next, a wall-mounted photo showed a young teenager in football jersey cradling a helmet embossed with a team logo.

"I see your son plays on the high school football team," said Rita with a cheerful tone and pointed over Roger's shoulder.

"Yes, offensive tackle."

Rita smiled.

"Weren't your son and Dingle's teammates at Lincoln High?" Vinnie followed Rita's lead.

"Until we moved to Ridgewood, yes."

"So they didn't remain friends even though they had been teammates?"

"No. Ken's been too busy training and they're, y'know, teenagers. Nothing's permanent."

The probing remained on football, the time and dedication necessary to play varsity. Roger reminisced about his own days in high school and at Princeton. "Competition was nothing like it is today."

Rita said she knew about training, and her earlier handshake gave the statement authenticity. She talked of supplements, diet, and the taboo subjects—human growth hormones, steroids, and diet drugs.

Vinnie interrupted, saying he could ask Ben for protein samples from his supplier for Ken but not juicing. "Can make a person a little crazy, you know, 'roid rage."

Rita jumped in, saying she'd seen young men and women go bonkers and asked if Roger worried about Ken. "You know, have you seen him act irrational at times?"

Roger shook his head, saying he didn't want to talk about his son, preferring to stay focused on the Lincoln High staff.

The interview meandered for another ten minutes. Vinnie told Roger if he didn't make more progress in two weeks he would close the investigation.

Afterward, Roger escorted Vinnie and Rita to the elevator and said, as if spontaneously, "I don't think your focus should be on the kids. This is about school politics, backbiting, backstabbing... schools aren't immune to that kind of crap."

"Yeah, right," said Vinnie to Rita as the elevator door closed, an edge to his voice. "I mean who fuckin' kills someone over a lunchroom assignment?"

A few blocks from Roger's office, in sight of the BIG building, Vinnie said, "I think it's time we talked to Brett."

***

"Didn't Dingle ask you to leave his son out of the investigation?" Blanca brought her morning coffee mug within slurping distance of her lips.

"Not in those exact words." Vinnie took a sip from his mug, staring out the office window. A strong wind blew the treetop branches. He turned as Blanca flexed her arms. "Okay, it was strongly implied."

"So how do we get his permission?"

Vinnie shrugged. "Your area of expertise, I think, what with you being a mother and all."

"And 'all'? What *all* am I?"

Vinnie sat at his desk, index finger to his lips. "What would persuade you to let your boys be interviewed?"

Blanca moved to the chair in front of Vinnie. "If I thought they were in danger."

"Then we'll go with that."

"What's the danger, pray tell?"

"Always the stickler for detail. Can't we just say they are 'in danger'?"

Blanca put her hands over her closed eyes.

Vinnie spoke like addressing a crowded room. "Let's say there's a mugging, unconfirmed, with local children witnessing the attack. Hint that we're concerned for Brett's safety. We fear the attacker believes Brett saw him or knows him. Maybe Brett had an encounter and hasn't told anyone or has suppressed it. Something like that."

Blanca uncovered her face, cheeks narrowing, hands supporting chin, moaning softly.

"What, you want it to be true?" Vinnie's voice chirped.

Blanca exhaled. They sat down together and a script of sorts took shape after fifteen minutes' deliberation, scattered with New York City pothole-size gaps.

"I'll try to set it up, but don't count on it." Blanca sounded exhausted.

After lunch she handed Vinnie a piece of paper. "What's this?"

"You'll need it for your GPS to get to the Dingle home."

"You are a wizard. Do you also do hexes?"

"Vinnie."

"Yes?"

"Here's a hex for you." Blanca held her middle finger up high. "Have a safe trip."

Chapter 10

Glen Dingle's initial solid negative dissolved as Blanca explained. "It's probably nothing, but our investigation revealed that after the first victim's attack a second attempt was made on the son." Blanca paused for Glen's deep inhale and exhale. Outright lying was her last resort. "Probably the attacker suspected the boy knew something. The police didn't follow up—"

"Sure," replied Glen Dingle.

And that single word was the reason why Vinnie and Rita found themselves in Mahwah. He was dressed in what he considered Jersey attire: khaki pants, brown belt, white socks, and a polyester short-sleeve no-iron shirt. "You're interviewing a high school student, not attending a reunion for engineers, class of 72," said Blanca, tutting.

Rita's outfit was the same Lycra form-fitting second skin she wore for Ken Bryant. "It works," she said in response to Vinnie's objection.

Brett Dingle was a few inches shorter than Ken Bryant but better looking and equally buff. Brett brought them to the living room, offering soda or water. He looked at Rita and suggested a high-energy sport drink. Vinnie said yes for both of them, explaining to Rita while Brett was in the kitchen that it was always good to accept an offer of refreshments as it slowed the interview process and gave them a chance to read the room. With a grin, he commented that Brett was a walking wet dream. Rita's tongue moistened her lips.

Condolences were dispensed to Brett, which he graciously acknowledged—a sharp contrast to Ken Bryant. Vinnie remarked on the beautiful house and neighborhood but got no reaction. Rita complemented Brett on his fitness and good looks, which elicited a shy smile.

The conversation roamed for ten minutes and Vinnie's eyelids drooped. Brett lounged, sipping on his sport drink, but sat bolt upright when Vinnie asked, "Can you tell us what happened at Lincoln High with Ken Bryant?"

Creases formed on Brett's forehead. "Nothing. I mean, we didn't mean it. It got out of hand. I was really sorry."

The silence lasted until Vinnie waved his hand as if seeking a sign of life.

"I, well, I mean Jeff was a little squirt. Snitching on Ken was so stupid. Ken and me could have broken him in two. He was lucky, really."

Rita's twisting brought a frown to Vinnie's countenance. Her small grumble seemed a prelude to pulverizing Brett's ass. Vinnie grabbed Rita's arms and as her fidgeting stopped, she said, "So, Jeff was lucky. And how would he know not to upset you and Ken?"

Vinnie edged forward as Brett answered. "Because unless Jeff is a complete retard, everyone at Lincoln knew not to mess with Ken, me, and the team. We could beat the entire freshman class to dust."

"And did you?" Rita's voice was sawdust dry.

Another long silence from Brett. Vinnie held on to Rita's arm to remind her to wait.

With a phlegmy throat clear, Brett's words stumbled out. "Look... we pushed kids into lockers... uh, teased some, punched a few arms in the hallway... nothing serious." He stopped to finish his drink. "Ken could go too far sometimes. I told him so." Brett covered his lips with both hands. "I didn't want to hurt anyone. Some kids I really liked. We used to be friends in grade school but they are too small to make the team, but they are okay I guess." Brett paused again, looking into his empty sport bottle as if willing it to fill. "I think we went too far with Jeff."

"How so?" Rita arched her back.

"What do you mean?"

"You didn't just tease Jeff or push him into a locker?"

"We just..." Brett stopped. "Ken went a little crazy is all."

Rita's nose snorted, and she sucked her cheeks in. "By a little, you mean multiple arm fractures, four cracked ribs, Jeff's face black and blue, broken nose, scratched cornea, spitting blood, kidney bruised, and in a hospital bed for five days? That kind of little?"

Brett froze, his eyes tearing, his lips tight, and visibly swallowing. "I think... uh... you should leave. I... uh... I have homework to do." Brett concealed his watering eyes with a backhanded swipe.

"Why, Brett? Something you don't want us to know about?" Rita stood, her breasts aimed at him. She knew their value. Her ex-boyfriend endlessly fondled them, tit-fucked them, approved of their shape, their hardness.

Watching Brett's stare, she squeezed her breasts together and studied his reaction. She knew the look. Her anger and frustration grew. She missed the rough sex with her ex. She liked his big dick pushing hard inside. Why did he leave, discard her? She looked at Brett. He would be someone's ex-boyfriend someday.

Her stance widened. After this interview she would troll the X-room to select a testosterone-supercharged stallion with gorilla stamina. Rita focused on the smug fresh meat in front of her. She wanted to fuck Brett's self-pity into genuine remorse. Rita moved closer to his button nose, give him a front row view of breasts bigger and harder than his.

Slipping across the room, Vinnie's lips brushed Brett's earlobe while whispering. The teenager's arm flung out and his hand twisted Vinnie's shirt collar. But if Brett was fast, Rita was faster. She brought her leg up with speed and precision to rest her heel on Brett's thigh, an inch from his crotch.

"You want kids one day? Release my partner or you'll be nursing your ruined gonads."

Brett released Vinnie, and his hand touched Rita's foot. Her tapping toes on Brett's thigh signaled him to remove his hand, which he placed on the seat cushion. His eyes were no longer on Rita's breasts but her mad-dog muzzle. He ordered them to get the fuck out of his fucking house or he'd call the fucking cops, but he sounded like a squeaky toy.

In the car, Rita turned to Vinnie. "What did you whisper to him?" Vinnie turned the steering wheel and eased the car from the curb.

"I told him that if he wanted to discuss coming out he could call me."

"What?!"

Vinnie looked both ways before proceeding through the intersection.

"How did you know?"

Vinnie grinned. "Remember your mother, the one that died when you were a teenager, not the one retired in Florida?" A deep belly laugh erupted from Vinnie. "Well... ha ha ha... I have gaydar that is sometimes right and sometimes not."

Rita smacked Vinnie's arm, causing the car to swerve. "You lying bastard."

***

The BIG office door banged against the wall, startling Blanca as Vinnie and Rita entered giggling. "This is going to be good, isn't it?"

"Uh-huh," said Rita.

Vinnie walked past Blanca dialing his cell and then asking Dan to come over when he was free. Around four-thirty Dan entered the BIG office with his laptop. He apologized for his lateness and offered an explanation but Vinnie interrupted, launching into a nonstop monologue about Ken and Brett, including clothing, appearance, attitude, and their homes.

After fifteen minutes of Vinnie's yammering, Blanca's yawn sounded like hissing air brakes. At the twenty-minute mark she interrupted, going to her office to call Al. On her return she announced her message as if it were a discovery of life on Mars. Her *el esposo* had supper ready for the hungry *niños*. She turned to Vinnie. "At your pace I'm here all night, so prepare a room with you and Ben. That okay by you?"

Vinnie looked like a dog sharing a water bowl.

"Hey, it's your lucky night *muy amor*." Blanca made kissing noises.

Vinnie stuck a finger down his throat, followed by Rita's smacking his head. He yelled out, "Ouch. That fuckin' hurt. Keep your fuckin' hands off me!"

Dan rubbed his chin and raised his eyebrows, making his face more handsome.

"I'm sorry, Dan, but that hurt."

Dan didn't dwell, accepting Vinnie's temporary cursing relapse. "What did Bryant and Dingle offer the injured boy's parents... er, what was his name?" he asked.

"Dellarosa. Jeff Dellarosa," said Rita.

"Okay, Dellarosa's parents," said Dan. "Why not press charges? Their son sustained significant injuries. He'll need long-term psychological help once his body heals. The assault was intended to inflict serious bodily harm. That's criminal, so even juvenile time is a possibility."

"I don't know." Vinnie looked around as if his lack of an answer was misplaced.

"Money, that's the usual thing." Blanca was in bare feet.

"How much are the Bryants and Dingles worth?" asked Rita.

Dan pushed aside his laptop. "I don't know about Dingle, but Roger Bryant handles wealthy trust funds. I'd guess he earns a lot of money. His clients are worth the GDP of a few small countries combined."

Vinnie's smile resembled someone passing wind.

Blanca waved her finger. "Let's get back to the boys. What about Brett Dingle? Why wasn't he suspended for the entire football season? Did his family pay a separate amount of hush money to Dellarosa's family or was it a package deal for both?"

"If we believe Brett, Ken was more culpable. Brett prevented Ken from killing Jeff Dellarosa, making Brett seem not as bad." Vinnie scrunched up his face.

"Should we talk to Dellarosa's parents?" Rita said, sitting forward.

Vinnie nodded. "A good idea but problematic if they were paid off. They'd have signed a confidentiality clause."

Ignoring the group's chatter, Vinnie drifted into his imaginary world. What to say about teenage thugs that evaded jail and continued to play football? *No fuckin' way the self-righteous athletic governing boards bother with trivia like violence. Disqualifications for drugs or an over-aged player or early college recruitment, sure. But for bullying? No fuckin' way.* Sweat formed on Vinnie's lips.

The meeting ended at seven when Dan rushed home to put his children to bed. Rita followed, saying she wanted to fit in a workout.

"Are you a robot or what?" Vinnie rolled his eyes.

Rita answered, "There are exercises to release stress if you know who to look for." The door closed behind her.

"*Who* to look for? It's *what* to look for, right?" Blanca pouted.

"Fuckin' A," said Vinnie, hitting his forehead with the palm of his hand. "*Who* to look for. That's it!"

Blanca stopped putting on her high heels. "Now you aren't making sense."

"The other day Dan told us to go wide and we did. Geographically, not victim wide."

"Vinnie, you become less coherent every day."

"We've looked at muggings among teachers because Alice Bryant and Emily Dingle were teachers. But they were also parents. What's the number of violent muggings among parents in middle- and upper-class neighborhoods?"

Blanca removed her shoes. "I'll be up for supper in an hour. Make my bed too."

"Yeah, yeah." Vinnie walked out with head lowered. How many murders would Blanca discover? He closed the office door as if it were made of fragile glass, wishing that Blanca would discover nothing, but he had never had much luck with wishes.

Chapter 11

The "no" from John Dellarosa interrupted Blanca before she could finish her sentence. His refusal was a battle cry—he and his wife had absolutely nothing to say. Blanca thought Mr. Dellarosa's condolences for the murdered woman were feigned and trite.

Two hours later, she made a second call and was thankful she reached Marie Dellarosa, who allowed Blanca to speak uninterrupted. Blanca emphasized Vinnie and Rita's sensitivity and guaranteed complete confidentiality. To Marie Dellarosa's enquiry about the BIG client's identity, Blanca replied that confidentiality went two ways.

Using Mrs. Dellarosa's delay as she thought about the response, Blanca moved on to the urgency in the matter by citing women at risk. The interview was to learn about motive and opportunity based on what happened at Lincoln High. "Wouldn't you like to help prevent more murders?" she asked plaintively.

Marie Dellarosa said she didn't understand. How could they help with the prevention of muggings and murders by talking about their son's incident? In Marie's words Blanca heard empathy, and she hated herself for what she had to say next. She described the murders in lurid detail, using brutal and horrific words. On the other end of the line Blanca heard Marie exhale like a punctured tire.

Blanca and Mrs. Dellarosa established ground rules: Jeff was excluded; Mr. Dellarosa's participation was doubtful; the interview stopped if it became unpleasant.

***

The modest new Morristown house looked small on its half-acre lot. Vinnie and Rita sank into the brownish-red couch, a checkered stain of spilt meals and beverages. Rita took small sips from her coffee mug while Vinnie gulped one-quarter of his. A plastic plate containing half a dozen donuts lay between two cardboard coasters on the coffee table in front of the couch. The food helped to smooth the awkwardness of the meeting.

Surprisingly, John Dellarosa had decided to be present, and he reclined in a Barcalounger throne facing an outsized wall-mounted flat-screen TV. An end table nestled against the chair for his mug. Marie Dellarosa sat in a small, white swivel chair positioned on the far side of the space. Sunlight streamed through an eight-foot-wide bay window yet failed to brighten up the enduring sense of misery in the room.

"I appreciate your meeting with us," began Vinnie, turning his head from John Dellarosa's hawk glare to Marie Dellarosa's morose, half-smiling face. "I know the memory is unpleasant and—"

"Unpleasant! They're a goddam nightmare," the man spat.

"John, please! Let Vinnie finish."

"It's okay, Marie, I understand. John has every right to be upset." Vinnie faced John's granite stare. A stocky, five-foot-five man, barrel chested with twisted ropes tattooed on his Popeye forearms. "John, I am truly sorry for what happened. I was bullied and beaten at school. Nothing like what happened to Jeff, but I had to change schools." Vinnie omitted that his father kicked him out of the house on learning he was gay. And the bully that beat him was his older homophobic brother whose career path finished with an eight-year stay at the Attica Correctional Facility.

The speech mollified John Dellarosa enough to dissolve his scowl, and his voice lowered to recognize Vinnie's sympathy. "It's a blow to the gut seeing your son beaten to within inches of death by big football jocks... no, *thugs*."

"You can't know," interrupted Marie looking into Vinnie's eyes, "how much it hurts as a parent to see your only son with fractures, a face so black and blue he was hardly recognizable beneath the bandages." She pulled a tissue from her pocket. "I'm sorry. I get emotional every time I think we might have lost our Jeff." She dabbed at her eyes.

"It's okay." Rita put down her mug on the cardboard coaster. She crossed her arms, preventing herself from twisting. "I train women and men to defend themselves against criminals who use their size to cause harm as if it's their God-given right."

Vinnie touched Rita's knee and she stopped, passing Vinnie the donut plate and waiting as he took one, then offered it to John Dellarosa. She was waved away as he said, "And their goddam money. Big shots. Earn on investments from our pension funds. They know where and how to invest their money. They earn while watching television or taking a shit." His voice cracked as he pointed at the wall-mounted TV. "They take home in a day more than what I take after a month of fifty-hour weeks sweating over a stove at the restaurant. Marie's on her feet for five hours a day checking-out groceries for $8.75 a goddam hour, barely over minimum wage. Then they buy us off!"

Neither Vinnie nor Rita spoke, not as a strategy but from shock. John Dellarosa had just confirmed the payoff.

"John, we're not supposed to... you know."

"Know what? Reveal we took money to keep our mouths shut? I think these two already know that. Am I right?"

"Yes," said Vinnie. "But that's not why—"

"Not here to shake us down? Be sure we don't talk by playing on our sympathy for the deaths of Mrs. Bryant and Mrs. Dingle? It won't work. They did nothing to stop their sons. Worse—they defended them. Gave us the boys-will-be-boys crap. I'm not grieving over their deaths. There, I said it. And I wish they would all—"

"Stop! John, don't say it." Marie turned to Vinnie and Rita. "We're upset. You know our son was nearly killed. He's had plastic surgery. He has nightmares. He sees a therapist. He's not the same. We moved to get him away from that school."

John joined in. "That's right. We bought this place using part of the settlement. Most goes to Jeff's counseling, rehab, private school tuition, and thirty percent to the lawyer." Mr. Dellarosa finally paused.

Marie's head bent and her eyes drooped, hand over her mouth. She looked up hearing her husband continue.

"Dingle couldn't make his share. He told us he was ashamed. Goddam hypocrite. Borrowed from Bryant, who probably wrote it off as a tax loss. They want their money back? Fuck them and fuck you too."

Marie shouted, "John, stop!" She wiped her lower eyelids again.

"I'm sorry," Vinnie said. "We're not here to shake you down. We do not represent Glen Dingle or Roger Bryant to renegotiate your settlement." Vinnie hoped the Dellarosas didn't catch the caveat. "We don't know the settlement details."

"I'll tell you." John looked to his wife wiping her eyes. He folded his arms. "Bryant turned over his son's college fund. Goddam broker had enough money fifteen years ago to open a college account the day his son was born. Amounted to a pretty penny. Dingle wasn't as clever. Even with his smaller payout... lawyer crap that his son 'was not as culpable' bullshit. Even so, Dingle couldn't come up with the money, not unless he sold his house. He cried poverty, said he had a second mortgage to support his business and blah blah blah."

Mr. Dellarosa leaned forward in his recliner. "We've enough for Jeff's tuition at the most expensive college but he's too fragile. He'll go to a local community college even though he's smart enough for Harvard."

Marie said she didn't want to talk about the money anymore. Vinnie agreed, moving on to the murders of Alice Bryant and Emily Dingle. He asked if they knew them before the attack. Marie said that she had met them a few times. Her impression was the women protected their sons more than their respective fathers. Marie believed she would defend Jeff more than her husband, which made John rock in his chair. "If my Jeff was involved in something wrong I'd have stopped him myself." His pointing finger speared into Vinnie. "But we taught Jeff right. To be a good person, not like those... scumbags. They and their families deserve to be shot!"

Marie shouted for her husband to stop again. She apologized, saying he didn't mean it, not the way it sounded. Vinnie nodded. Told her not to worry, he understood that John's anger did not mean action. The interview concluded after a few more words as if it were a friendly visit, but a thinly veiled bitterness lingered.

Marie walked Vinnie and Rita to the front door. Rita remarked on the beautiful flowers in the hall entrance.

"Yes, they are. A local florist delivers a fresh bouquet once a week at no charge."

"Why do they do that?" Vinnie asked.

"Don't know. Kindness, maybe." She giggled, which took Rita by surprise. "The company supplies flowers to various school functions around Bergen County. The owner heard about Jeff from the secretary at Lincoln High, who gave him our address. Aren't they beautiful?"

***

Waiting in a two-mile traffic line on Route 3 before the GW Bridge tolls, Vinnie and Rita analyzed their interview. Vinnie recalled John Dellarosa's comment that Jeff wouldn't do illegal stuff, unlike the two privileged bullies whose parents didn't seem to give a damn. Vinnie took his hands off the steering wheel, wagging his index fingers upward, "Maybe Jeff wouldn't do anything illegal before but if he's as messed up as Marie says, he's doing drugs now."

"Cynical much?" Rita chugged her water, dehydrated from the interview.

"Realistic. Get serious." Vinnie believed they needed more on the Lincoln incident, as he dubbed it. He was sure Bryant would not cooperate, leaving just Dingle. The problem was Dingle chewed Blanca out on hearing about Brett's interview. Threatened legal repercussions. "Lucky Glen never met you. Can you do an undercover interview?"

Rita giggled. "Undercover has never been a problem." Her laugh rose until she saw Vinnie chewing his lower lip. "Chill. I'll get what you want, trust me."

Chapter 12

"She'll be furious when she sees this," Blanca said to Vinnie while reading Ken and Brett's private Facebook messages thanks to Katy Bryant's slip revealing her brother's password: "bigbadmotherfucker."

Ken's sexist and misogynist postings were no surprise to Blanca and Vinnie. He spent an inordinate amount of time deconstructing Rita's body from head to toes, but mostly focusing on her boobs, ass, and vagina as if doing a warehouse inventory. The boys joked over what they would do to each part of her body—a series of crude, misogynistic vulgarities. Their sexual prowess was manifestly unimpressive in Blanca's opinion and Vinnie agreed. Blanca choked while reading out loud Ken's view that Rita was not as bad as some of the girls in his school, so he'd forgo putting a bag over her head while he fucked her. Brett wrote that it wasn't a problem for him, as he just planned to fuck her up the ass.

Vinnie tapped Blanca's monitor. "Let's keep this from Rita, shall we? It won't help her interview Glen, and on the off-chance she meets Brett, well, let's say we might have a new case searching for the body."

"Vinnie, it's risky if it comes out."

"What's risky if what comes out?" said Rita, whose entry made Blanca and Vinnie blush as if caught in an amorous embrace.

"Uh... oh, Rita, I... I thought you had a tae kwon do class today." Vinnie smiled like a billboard poster for cheap toothpaste.

"Cancelled. The room's being fumigated because someone brought two dogs crawling with fleas into the place. Ben turned more rainbow colors than a Gay Pride Parade and issued a lifetime ban."

Vinnie sulked. Ben would not be approachable tonight.

"So, what's this about something being risky?" Rita moved behind Blanca to see the computer screen.

Seeing Blanca's raised eyebrows, Vinnie conceded with a shrug to Rita. Blanca gave her the summary: Brett's and Ken's Facebook messages demeaned women. Rita gummed her lips. She waited until Blanca flipped the screen to the Facebook page, at which point Vinnie backed away.

Solar flares shot from Rita's eyes. Her cursing impressed Vinnie. She crouched, fighter's stance, fists forming.

Vinnie placed his palms together like a preacher. "I think we should rethink your interview with Glen."

Rita stopped jabbing the air, but her lips puckered like she was inflating a balloon. Veins surfaced on her forehead. "I'll be fine," she said with a menacing tone.

"And if you meet Brett?"

"Why would I? I'm going to Glen's office. And if I do I'll be professional."

"Right, no problem," said Vinnie, his words blowing air. "But if Brett sees you, do we call a riot squad? Look at your reaction just now. Too risky."

Tapping her computer screen with a long fingernail, Blanca interrupted. "On rereading this crap, the really offensive comments are from Ken more than Brett."

Rita took the mouse from Blanca's hand to scroll the screen. "Brett's comment here." She read out loud. "I'd push my dick so far into her cunt I'll be able to grab the end of it as it comes out her hard ass."

Blanca tilted her head. "That one's not good, but Ken's are worse—"

Rita's grumble resembled an engine room.

"Okay," said Blanca with head shaking, "I think we can all agree that both are immature and disrespectful." She pointed to the screen. "But look closer. Brett's comments echo Ken's or respond to his encouragement. That was the exception."

Rita read more of the exchange. She crouched lower, cursing, taking a chair and then flinging it across the room.

Vinnie cancelled Rita's interview with Glen. With hands chopping the air, she argued, cursed, and slapped the desk. She looked to Blanca, who wagged two index fingers side to side. "You agree with him?" Rita scoffed.

"He's the boss, and this is his agency." Not an entirely true statement as Blanca held private shares, but shares aside, Vinnie was the driving force behind BIG. "And look at yourself. I don't blame you, but you are going ballistic."

Rita's sneakers left rubber marks on the wooden floor from her rapid departure.

"Thanks for supporting me. Did you know Rita fucked another X-room guy last night?"

Blanca's mouth dropped open.

"Come on. Ben hears things. He feels responsible for pushing Rita to join us, and worries it was too soon. He figures something's going on in her head. She's been stalking guys at UltraFit since her breakup. He'd ban her, but she's too fragile. And it's not like she sells drugs." Vinnie smiled. "I hear the guys are cool with her. Duh!" Vinnie laughed while Blanca glared at him. "Okay, Ben's worried others might follow Rita's action, turning the X-room into 'the X Room.' Let me tell you, one guy said Rita can—"

Blanca turned off her computer, grabbed her coat, and went for something to eat, leaving Vinnie mid-sentence.

***

The call came as Blanca returned from her long lunch. Dan was on the line telling her he had crunched more numbers on a bigger spreadsheet using data he discovered in his online research. He asked Blanca to check for murdered high school staff over the last year at private high schools.

A full afternoon's digging produced the projected results, yet she was still shocked. One obituary without the cause of death listed, not even the bland "after a short illness." The woman had retired nine months earlier from a religious-affiliated high school.

Blanca updated Vinnie with Dan's new assignment for obits without death attribution. "With diseases the family often request donations to a charity. But to print nothing... why?" Blanca lowered her chin and rubbed her fingernails.

"Dunno. Maybe too painful? Respect for the departed? If it was a violent death, to not give the uncaught attacker satisfaction?" Vinnie scratched his head. "I agree with Dan. Let's dig up more deaths."

Blanca closed her eyes, grunting at Vinnie's words. He ignored her "wrong words" comment, and held his head with both hands. "Oh no."

"What?" Blanca reached to grasp Vinnie's arm.

"There will be more. This hasn't stopped," he said.

Blanca stood back. "When? Where?" She looked around for lurking danger.

"Not the right questions. We need to get to the bottom of this. We need to find out the 'why.' And that with tell us the 'who.'"

Blanca rubbed her arms as if walking along the frozen food aisle of a supermarket.

"Check Facebook messages of our two favorite macho football jocks. Go further back, but beyond messages between them to include among their teammates too." Vinnie looked over his shoulder. "Um, maybe get Al's help too."

Jeopardizing her husband's computer profession to hack on Vinnie's behalf wasn't kosher with Blanca. She grumbled her displeasure. "Besides, what am I looking for?" she concluded.

"You'll know when you see it."

"Oh masterful one, you have a real knack for team guidance."

***

The next day Vinnie discovered that his guidance did indeed prove masterful. Blanca was beaming as she leaned into him. "You owe Al big-time." She gestured throwing an imaginary baseball, which Vinnie understood meant he'd be buying box seats at a Mets game. "You'll never guess what came up on my wild goose chase through the sea of crap that is Facebook?"

"The point of you doing it was so I don't have to guess."

"*Culo.*"

"Nice change-up. I love it when you talk dirty in a foreign language."

After telling him to shut his mouth and drop the running commentary, she disclosed her discovery. Private messages to Ken Bryant from his teammates praised him for beating that "little shit Jeff Dellarosa." Disgust spread across her face as the foul language increased. Ken's reply varied, but overall he gloated, sounding proud and pompous: "I fucking showed him." "Felt so good I creamed my pants." "My biggest hard-on ever from pulverizing that puny punk." "Taught the faggot a lesson. Showed him what fucking muscles can do."

The messages stopped after Ken and Brett's arrest, then started again following the Bryants' moved to Ridgewood. The meaning was intended to be cryptic, but Blanca had no trouble reading between the teenagers' lines. Praise continued for Ken, mostly about him getting away with it.

"Here's the one to read." Blanca scrolled her screen and waited for Vinnie, which didn't take too long given the short but clear message.

"Fuckin' unbelievable." Vinnie threw his arms in the air.

"Yes. My thoughts exactly."

"That might be the reason. Cross-check for something unusual in other cases." Vinnie touched the computer monitor.

Blanca looked at Vinnie. "Like I said yesterday, masterful guidance."

Vinnie's smile widened,

"Yup, pile it on. One more thing for me to do." Blanca matched Vinnie's dental display. "There's something needs doing and it won't be me doing it."

A rush of air escaped from Vinnie. "Me? My plate's full."

"Not you; Rita. She has to interview Glen Dingle."

Vinnie's body nearly folded in half. Blanca threw her pen onto her desk. "Stop it. We need her to confirm. It can't be you, so it has to be Rita. I don't care how she does it but she needs to get the information. And she needs to think this a joint decision, *capisce?*"

With a roll of his eyes, Vinnie turned, muttering that her Italian had declined as he walked to his desk to retrieve his cell phone. From his grumble Blanca knew he disagreed and she rushed ahead to grab his handset before he could make the call. "Better let me." With a small peck to his forehead she said, "You're adorable when you're so agreeable."

Vinnie slammed the door behind him as Blanca phoned Rita.

Chapter 13

Fury lingered and no amount of yoga reduced Rita's tension. She admitted as much to Blanca on hearing the Glen Dingle interview was on again. Brett and Ken's objectification stung as well. Too often the term hypocrite had been thrown at her—wasn't bodybuilding narcissistic, with every sinew objectified? Why care now? But she did. The boys were different.

In Rita's mind, contest spectators differed from the general public, and much more compared to the two teenagers. Fitness fans knew how to look and what to look for, in a way that ballet audiences considered the synergy of strength, athleticism, and choreography in a dancer's performance.

A sculpted body had never been Rita's teenage goal, her "hell years." Being tall didn't hide her excess weight, earning her various "fatty" sobriquets. She endured whispering voices in corridors and locker rooms, but was spared social media taunts as the World Wide Web was a few years away. The words hurt because they were accurate. Saturated fat slalomed its way down Rita's gullet: hamburgers, fries, pizza, donuts. But Rita was never bullied; no one dared or she'd roll over onto them.

At high school graduation she ported five foot nine inches, one hundred ninety-five pounds up five stage stairs to the dais, sucking air, reaching for her diploma from the principal.

A freak car accident as a college freshman nearly killed her and everything changed. Six months of physiotherapy included weight training and a low-calorie diet. Rita dropped twenty pounds. During rehab she avoided fast food. The therapy continued at the college gym. By sophomore year she ran five miles daily, and switched to a "real" gym, which in her opinion meant grime and large sweaty men—no women. The burly, brick-chewing owner trained Rita. She exchanged twenty-five pounds of fat for twenty of muscle. She carted herself on campus with thunder legs, a size six body, an eye-popping chest, and sinewy arms. Men noticed, and she liked it.

In her senior year Rita became a serious bodybuilder. The taunting returned, this time for her "disgusting bulges." Her roommates begged her to stop, but Rita's goal was to lift a quarter-ton and turn professional. At her college graduation she mounted the dais three stairs at a time, leaping on the stage to cheers. She could have carried off the dean and her diploma under one powerful arm.

As a pro-bodybuilder, Rita forfeited any steady job. Her life vacillated between waitressing and training. Ben discovered her during a New York City contest. He offered Rita a position as UltraFit's martial arts instructor, access to private clients, no dues, and he would be her personal trainer in the exclusive X-room with the goal being a first-place trophy.

Rita surveyed the X-room like an explorer discovering man continents for the first time. She studied their flexing, grunting, and cursing. Watching the men pump, she craved a good fuck. Sexual desire increased with her gain. Her choice in men was eclectic: big and small; fit and flabby; big dicks and tiny ones. If she achieved multiple climaxes, the man earned a second or third date. For most, the *adios* came after one disappointing screw.

Her reputation for bone-crunching sex became UltraFit's urban legend. She had several nicknames, all known to Vinnie: Barbarella; She-Woman; Valkryie; Sperm Churner. With her first proper boyfriend, Rita's world changed. The ravenous sex rampages diminished. Affection, attachment, and bonding wrapped into fidelity made the sex better. Her first experience with love had more impact on her emotional state than all the shrinks combined, better even than Ben during their weight-training sessions. But when her lover dumped her, the old drive and the old habits soon returned. She knew this would make interviewing Glen Dingle difficult. Vinnie had described the man as "absolutely drop-dead gorgeous, a hunk twice over." As far as Rita was concerned, he could have said the interview was with a tree, as long as it had a penis.

Rita decided this was the time to develop her unique interview style. She planned to extract information from Mr. Heartthrob with side benefits for herself.

***

Parking her rental car in the visitors' bay of the Fair Lawn Office Park, Rita searched the signs for the building with Glen Dingle's office.

"Hello and welcome to Barnetto and Dingle," said the receptionist seated at a modern glass desk, soft drink to her side. She chirped, "How may I help you?" Rita thought the thin woman needed a seatbelt to stay in the grown-up chair.

"I have an appointment with Mr. Dingle." Rita stopped herself from stretching.

"And you are?"

"Rita Moreno." Rita sniggered at Vinnie's suggested pseudonym, keeping her first name and substituting a famous actor's surname. Blanca applauded the use of the famous Puerto Rican actress of *West Side Story* fame.

"Please have a seat. I'll let Mr. Dingle know you're here." Rita declined a soft drink offer and hung her winter overcoat on the coat stand.

"Mr. Dingle will only be a few minutes. His conference call began late."

Rita didn't mind. She specifically asked for the last appointment of the day, allowing for a leisurely interview without concern for the next client.

She saw the tall man walking her way from a distance. As he approached, Rita thought his belt a notch too tight, which only a fitness judge would notice. His upright posture stiff, like a plank with swinging arms. Raising his hand in greeting, Rita noticed his shirt's fabric pull to outline his pectorals. As he neared, Rita's lips puckered as if to whistle at this most handsome man, so much more than Vinnie's meager "He's a good-looking guy" comment. Rita would pin his photo to her bedroom wall or, better still, him.

His warm smile, deep voice, and dark complexion made her think of fudge sundae and she licked her lips. "Glen Dingle. Sorry for the delay. Shall we go to my office, Ms. Moreno?"

"Please, call me Rita."

"Okay. I'm Glen. Very pleased to meet you." If he had asked, she would have ripped off her clothes and let him do whatever he wanted right there in front of the receptionist; then she would return the favor. *I'm for equality between the sexes.* These were the first of several lascivious thoughts she had walking behind him.

In Glen Dingle's office, she placed her Forty-Second Street vendor's knockoff briefcase on the floor, bending to withdraw a folder, then stretched to hand it to Glen. The folder contained Blanca's carefully crafted financial portfolio for the fictitious Moreno Woman's Fitness Center, cribbing data from the Briggs Investigative Group accounts. Glen gestured for Rita to keep the folder.

"First, let's talk about your business and what you are looking for in an accounting firm." His deep, creamy voice mesmerized Rita. "Number-crunching is the easy part. I try to match my service to a client's needs." In his pause, Rita considered vaulting the desk and nailing Glen in his leather chair. "Can you tell me about your business, and your previous experience with an accounting firm?" He steepled his finger under his chin. "Especially if you are switching firms. I'd like to know why?"

His questions were logical and reassuring, and all anticipated. Yet she shuffled in her seat as if not knowing where to place the folder. The movement rustled her tight-fitting, low-cut blouse over her ample bosom. Taking her time, she replaced the folder in the briefcase, crossed her legs, and sat upright. The movement explained her previous experience. Now to explain the change in accountants.

"Well, I'm expanding basically," Rita illustrated with a large inhale, back arching that in turn uplifted her breasts. "My brother-in-law does my bookkeeping, but he's an amateur. He thinks Quicken makes him an expert." Rita took another deep breath, her chest encroaching on Glen's desktop. "And, to be perfectly honest, he tells my sister everything. She's too judgmental about how I run my business."

Rita gave Glen time to eye-stroll her tits. He leaned back, getting comfortable. "I understand." Rita was sure he didn't.

"My plan is to hire ten employees in the coming months, adding to my current roster of three. The additional Federal and State tax paperwork and an employee health package will be tricky." Rita followed the script prepared by Blanca and Vinnie.

She wondered if Glen was smiling in agreement or just happy with his view. The buzzing phone interrupted them.

"Sure, that's okay, Karen. I'll lock up after I finish with Rita... Ms. Moreno."

The discussion wandered. Rita quizzed Glen on his qualifications and background. He disclosed more than he had intended. His accounting degree from Penn State and his time as a Nittany Lions quarterback—"We made it to the Bowl." He had married a girl from college—he paused with no further explanation or reference but Rita could tell from what little he said that she was dead, even though she already knew the fact. After 9/11, he and his business partner left their New York firm to branch out on their own in Jersey. He had one son who played varsity football on the high school team. No pets and mortgage paid.

Rita nodded. "I'm not surprised you were a college football player, given your size."

"It's been a while since I was in my youth." He touched his waist. "I've put on weight in all the wrong places. I work out as often as my schedule permits, or I'd be all flab."

"You're too modest. Look at you. Youthful and trim. I know something about fitness." Rita gave a short laugh. "That's my business and reason for being here, isn't it?" She knocked his desk for good luck. "Women like my methods but they also work for men."

"I'll bet they do. You look *terrific*."

Was he being coy? Rita held her thoughts. Handsome. Modern hairstyle. Neat eyebrows emphasizing his long lashes. Friendly smile displaying teeth yet non-aggressive. A delicate nose between symmetrical, high cheekbones crowning wide lips. "Gosh, it's after six. Have I stayed too long?" Her last words a silky simper.

"Don't worry. This consult is free, including the overtime." His hearty laugh was a little too obvious. She saw that he was interested in her, and not just for bookkeeping.

Rita twisted a quarter-turn, leaned forward, her breasts brushing the desk, resting her arms, hushing her words as if telling a secret. "I appreciate it, but I don't want your charity—"

Glen interrupted Rita, edging forward in his chair. "It's not. It's a courtesy for all potential clients." Glen's eyes dropped again.

Rita sat back, preparing to reel in her tuna. "I'd love to show my appreciation. Are you free for dinner? I'm starving and I don't know this neighborhood."

As he locked the building entrance, he walked to his car while Rita ambled to hers. Using her car's side mirror, a technique she taught women before unlocking their doors, she saw Glen watching her.

Time to go off script.

Chapter 14

The upscale Italian restaurant was close to Glen's home. Rita kept to her diet, ordering a large salad, fish, boiled potatoes, two sides of beans, and plenty of water. She accepted one glass of wine from Glen's expensive Sauvignon Blanc.

She surprised Glen and made him laugh when she said the portions were meager for bodybuilders. He laughed like a delighted child, and Rita knew she liked Glen Dingle more than she should. Maybe it was the wine or her being horny, but she thought he had become more attractive in the last couple of hours.

"Shall we have coffee at my place? Give us a chance to work this off?" he asked, his eyebrows shooting up. Rita heard his laugh and watched him pat his stomach to cover the gaffe. She didn't care. Beneath his innuendo-laced tone she heard the sadness.

"I'd like that. You sure it's not inconvenient? I mean, with your son?"

"Brett will be fine. He should be doing homework but he'll be chatting or texting or whatever the hell they do online these days. I'm the last thing on his mind." Glen's voice lost its lilt.

Rita wanted to shout the truth. His son's online chat demeaned women. Demeaned her. She twisted but stopped as Glen continued in his subdued voice. "To be honest, I don't keep up. My wife, Emily... well, she monitored his homework and school stuff."

Glen's voice dipped into the region called despair. His tone had gone quiet as they sat motionless while he talked about his wife. Rita rested her forearms on the table. He should have explained before they entered the restaurant, let her know this wasn't a sordid assignation. But he didn't. He picked up his napkin, his gold wedding ring reflecting light from the candle on the table. Rita stared a little too long, unintentionally, so he put his hand under the napkin. He assured Rita that this dinner was not cheating because Emily was dead.

Rita feigned surprise at the news, but her sympathy was sincere. Glen made a point that he had never cheated on Emily and this was his first supper alone with another woman since it happened.

He became somber as they walked to the parking lot, a sharp contrast to their jovial banter during the meal. Rita thought he might rescind his offer of coffee, and needed him to volunteer. "Are you up for me coming to your place? If not, I completely understand." She wanted to say, *If yes, I plan to fuck your brains out in the next phase of the interview*. She was way off script. Vinnie would be furious if she told him, her excuse lame. "I took your advice," interpreting his parting words literally: "Just do a fuckin' good interview." Glen said it was fine, and appeared to cheer up as she got into her car to follow him home.

***

After a short drive Glen waved Rita into the open bay of the three-car garage beneath a large, modern house split into two wings. Rita hesitated as the garage door closed. "You sure we won't disturb your son?"

"Brett won't know we're here." Glen's architectural description of the house layout assured her that the garage staircase was nowhere near Brett's bedroom. She thought the detailed description was offered up as much to assure himself as her. *He probably called Brett to be sure he was in his room.*

The coffee was put on hold as Rita requested a tour of the house, specifically the master bedroom and en suite bathroom—she needed to pee. She emerged sans coat, blouse, trousers, bra, and panties. Glen's jaw gaped at Rita's naked body, her deep and even tan looking like she'd been dipped in chocolate, her rippling muscles accentuated by the dimmed bedroom lights. She heard Glen calling her a goddess in faltering words. She stood with hands behind her back, legs crossed, and watched his eyes trawl her teardrop thighs and torpedo breasts. Her flexing was awkward, too many years since the exhibition days, yet memory-muscle quickly returned. Her double-bicep pose felt jerky. She worried her guns were unimpressive, knowing they lacked the size and definition of her time on the competition circuit.

"Jesus, Rita, that's incredible," sputtered Glen. "How long have you been working out? I mean, *Christ.*"

She walked closer, held her pose, and waited. Glen took hold of her biceps. "Fuck, these are like rocks."

Lowering her arms, she unbuckled his belt. "Now let's see what you've got down here."

Without protest, he stood, allowing his pants to fall to his ankles, while his tented undershorts spoke for him. Rita ripped his shirt and stretched his underwear over his elongated cock. He would need twenty-four hours to roll his tongue back into his mouth and his impressive priapism to recede.

If Glen was excited by Rita, she felt the same on seeing his toned body and hardened penis. Dipping her forehead under his chin she rubbed his sinewy arms and spreading deltoids. His arm reached around Rita, squeezing her ass tight. Rita reciprocated, with one hand pinching his stomach, pleased it was not flab and that the over-tightened belt was unnecessary. She clawed at his buttocks while her free hand snaked between his legs, a single finger circumnavigating his balls as if etching her name. She imagined his testicles engorged from months of unspent semen, unless of course he self-released. His groan suggested not. He was a twelve-gauge shotgun ready to unload.

With his embrace her skin warmed, as if encased by a wool blanket. She planned to fuck Glen until he shriveled inside her. She circled her labia with his penis as if applying lipstick. With a leap, her legs wrapped around Glen's waist, her ass crack atop his hard cock; the move nearly toppled them.

"Let's start with FPF."

"Huh?"

"Don't worry, you'll catch on." Rita had melded yoga and martial arts into sexual positions, inventing names from traditional positions. Fe-Pe-Fuck or Feathered Peacock Fuck derived from the Pincha Mayurasana Yoga Happiness pose.

Glen stayed quiet, astounded as Rita maneuvered to hang inverted, her legs wrapping around his neck, her pussy pressed to his face, and both her hands crimped his ass like a rock climber. With slow steps, Glen marched backward until his ass hit the bed's edge. Rita shouted "OFF" to catapult upward, her legs resting on Glen's shoulders, her pussy mashing his face, his voice muffled by her labia.

"Mmph?"

"OFF. Open the Fan Fuck. Don't stop." This was among Rita's favorite tai chi poses.

Rita saw Glen's pumpkin-size eyes surveying her Brazilian wax. She suspected he had only seen a naked pussy online recently. She moved her exposed clitoris inches from his nose.

His tongue extended, the tip barely reaching her labia, with her tits resting on his head, his eyes staring at her navel. His small nose inhaling her fragrance excited her. She was moist and ready for him.

As if Glen were an unbroken mustang, Rita pulled his nape to whisper in his ear, "Lo-Sho-Fuck: Lotus in Shoulder Fuck." She tilted Glen's head, sliding her legs down around his waist, one tit jammed in his face forcing him to suckle until he couldn't breathe. He gasped, toppling back, and the two fell on the bed. Glen shuffled the full length and spread his legs. Rita turned over to invite rear entry for his penis. He saw the reverse of her Brazilian, her Con Edison hole. Glen cried out that he was ready and Rita asked, "Where's the cream?"

"Oh, fuck, I threw it out."

Rita moved off, went into the bathroom and returned with hair conditioner. "Let's try this." She liked the musky, tangy smell of men's body products: aftershave, cologne, deodorant, and soap.

With a slathering worthy of Jiffy Lube, she covered Glen's penis, belly, and frothed his balls for fun. Fully lubricated, Glen barreled into Rita's vagina. She lifted herself with him on top. Glen called out, "How? This is impossible."

With a laugh, she answered, "Not for me and Mod-Feather-Puck-Fuck, using a modified feathered peacock position. Now make me preen."

She pounded and Glen yelled out, "I can't hold it."

Rita slipped out, pinching Glen's balls. His eyes popped but not his penis. "Better?"

"Uh-huh..."

"Then let's try Dove."

"I... what?"

"Dove Fuck."

Glen complied, still confused. She nudged him, creating space to roll, her legs sprouted to the ceiling. On cue, Glen aimed and hit the bull's-eye.

"Wait," said Rita. Her legs spread, a weft of sinew and stomach rippled. With the power of a stone crusher, she squeezed Glen, crying out unfamiliar words as an incantation to his pumping ejaculation.

"That was incredible." Glen caught his breath, laying flat on the bed with an arm propping his head. Rita nuzzled into him.

"Good?"

"Good? That was just... I don't know. You're like a cannon and Emily was more of a firecracker." His face turned dark. "I don't mean it that way. I loved Emily. Our sex was good. But that was... different."

With a warm grin Rita kissed Glen, pinching his nipples. She rested her back on the headboard. Glen turned onto his stomach, propping himself up on his elbows, staring at her face.

"You are the strongest woman I've ever known." He sat upright. "Want a drink?" Glen walked naked, body shining, perfect, a man unlike any Rita had ever known. He bent to a cabinet, and she admired his ass and legs, even though it was nothing like the iron girders strutting around the X-room. But Glen was more than muscle fiber. *Knows how to look, that's the difference*, she thought.

She accepted the drink, yet reminded him she had to drive home. She refused his offer to stay the night, not telling him the risk of meeting Brett was too high.

Glen sat sideways on the bed, handing Rita a glass with an inch of Scotch whisky in it and his filled twice as much. They clinked glasses. Glen took a large gulp while Rita sipped. It had been a long time since she had hard liquor. The bitter taste returned her to her purpose.

"Is Brett into this?" She held up her glass. "Don't you worry, with no one home to monitor his drinking?"

"Yeah, a little. But he is into his sports drink and high-protein shakes. Right now he's concentrating on getting bigger and stronger. He trains nonstop. You should meet him. He's six foot and two hundred. He'll get bigger in college. He's had offers, but a scholarship's irrelevant, with Emily's insurance—" Glen stared into his glass. He gulped the rest then got up to pour a refill.

Rita admired his muscular legs again, the firm buttocks, his good looks. She stared at his penis as he returned to the bed. "It's hard, isn't it? I mean..." She laughed and Glen joined her without a hint of his earlier anxiety.

"Not like before, but you never know." Glen wiggled his flagging penis, his masculine laugh pleasing Rita. She liked him, despite wanting to hate his guts. She came for an inquisition and sex, and had only completed one of the objectives. It was time to return to the mission, but empathy over the man's murdered wife deflected her. He didn't deserve to have his wife killed, nor for that matter did Emily deserve to be murdered. No one did.

"Is he a good football player?" Rita forced herself to act as if she liked Brett.

"Good, but nothing super. He acts like he is but I was on a Big Ten team and he wouldn't cut it there. To be honest, Brett shoots his mouth off. He has too high an opinion of himself." Rita thought, *you have that right*. Glen took a long swig of his Scotch, draining half the glass. His eyes drooped.

Rita evaluated, considered another few minutes to allow the alcohol-infused bloodstream to soften Glen's brain. She continued to talk, pretending to understand the immaturity of macho male teenagers. Moving to kneeling position behind Glen, she pressed her breasts into his back, wrapping her hands around his chest. She nibbled his earlobe, one hand massaged his chest, the other a lover's caress to his manhood. In ten minutes she heard about the Lincoln High bullying case.

"Geez, how awful. You must have been beside yourself."

"Yeah, although Emily always defended him. Said it was the other kid's fault."

"Who?"

"A teammate, someone called Ken Bryant. He was permanently kicked off the team. Glen received a one-season suspension."

A few hours remained before daybreak and the roads were empty. Rita's return drive was smooth, but she knew that would change on arrival. How to summarize for Vinnie the information without revealing her interview method?

Chapter 15

"Fuckin' unbelievable." Vinnie shifted back and forth in his swivel chair. Blanca's right-hand index finger shot up next to her extended thumb. All five fingers of her left hand outstretched as if expecting to be gloved.

"Just fuckin' unbelievable."

Up went Blanca's middle finger. "Eight." She didn't think Vinnie would make fourteen, his personal best. His speech slowed.

"I mean, *fuckin'* unbelievable."

Her ring finger shot up. "Nine. Are you finished?" Blanca was tired of holding up her hands. She thought nine "fuckin' unbelievables" excessive. "Let Rita continue. I'd like to do some work before it's time to go home."

Vinnie stopped moving in his chair. "I want to make this very clear. Rita does not see or talk to Glen Dingle. Understood? We do not screw to gain information." Vinnie was taking deep breaths. "Do you get it?"

"Yes. But I did—"

"It doesn't matter. A case becomes compromised when you screw someone we are investigating."

With her head and eyes lowered, Rita chewed her lip. She balled her hand and her arms tightened.

Blanca's words pelted Vinnie. "Enough. We all agree sex is not an interview method. Satisfied? Now let's hear about what Rita learned."

Rita abridged her encounter, thinking she would later confide to Blanca about the sex. Athletic, glorious sex, making her ex-boyfriend's performance pale in comparison. She was disingenuous. The ex was good, his equipment impressive, yet nothing compared to Glen or his consideration. *Sleazy bastard, cheating, goddam, son-of-a-bitch fucker of an ex-boyfriend.*

"We were in his bedroom—" Rita gasped as Vinnie screamed.

"You were in his house? Not the car or a motel? What if Brett saw you? *Fuckin' unbelievable!*" Vinnie turned to see if Blanca's pinky was elevated.

"Enough, Vinnie. Let Rita finish." With arms folded, Blanca's head tilted back to Rita.

"We were careful. Brett's room is located on the opposite side of the house. Glen wanted to avoid being seen too."

Rita's narrative was a convoluted story of mortgage loans and Emily's wealthy father's advance that enabled the one-point-five-million Dingle home purchase. An added home-equity helped Glen invest in his partnership. Then catastrophe struck Emily's father. He lost his entire portfolio and two homes to the financial swindler Bernie Madoff. The Dingles re-mortgaged to enable Emily's parents to retire to a fifteen-hundred-square-foot Florida condo, leaving the Dingles cash-strapped.

"Geez, I'm feelin' so sad for them I might just *cry*," said Vinnie with lips puckered.

Blanca tapped her backside and told Rita to "Ignore the *pendejo*."

Weaving in and out of her story Rita struggled to pass over the sex and her narrative became confusing. Vinnie lost the thread a few times but got the big picture: Glen Dingle didn't have a pot to piss in when hit with the civil and criminal lawsuit by the Dellarosa family. He would have lost everything—his home, savings, and business. Glen felt shamed accepting Roger Bryant's money but had no choice. Roger too resented the payment and had no choice; the deal depended on a joint settlement for both boys.

"How do you know this? And bailed out how?" Vinnie was leaning on his elbows, eyes drilling into Rita's.

Blanca had moved to stand beside Vinnie. Rita turned to the window behind Vinnie and Blanca.

"We were in his bed and he opened up. Told me everything." She stopped.

The image played in her mind. Glen's ass pressed against the bedroom wall and her performing an OLWF—One-Legged Wheel Fuck. The heel of her right foot on Glen's shoulder as she stood on her left, the two legs forming a line from floor to wall. He had been deep inside her, hands grasping her ass as he thrust. His fingers sunk into her anus as pulled himself further inside. Their simultaneous climax caused a crash to the floor. In contrast to her euphoria, tears ran along Glen's cheeks. He sobbed into her neck. He needed to confess.

Rita continued with her reverie. She knew she was a good fuck, but this had meant more than sex to Glen—it was his return to the living. She also knew he would cry again when realizing he would never be with her, but at that moment she had been his intimate confidante. He told her everything. She wanted to reciprocate, but it was impossible. She too would cry. She wanted Glen forever. He could have been her future, her shutting the door on the past. She wanted him not for carnal lust, although she wanted that, but for his essence, and knowing he needed her in the same way. Isn't that what love is about?

"We could sit here all day and try to read your mind, or you could just tell us," Vinnie's voice rasped. Blanca reached over and twisted his earlobe. "Hey, that hurt!"

"Shut up. Can't you see this is hard for Rita? She didn't just have sex with Glen, she likes him."

"*Bull*shit."

Blanca turned to Rita, pointing her thumb at Vinnie. "Like I said, a big asshole. Grand *pendejo*."

Rita wiped her eyes, refocused from the window to Vinnie. "Well, in his bed... okay, that's irrelevant. What matters is that Glen said he couldn't believe he knew three murdered people. I asked if he knew more about the guy... Bob... uh—"

Vinnie interrupted. "Reinhardt? The dead hunter?"

"Yeah. Glen said it happened late September nearly a year before Emily's murder. No one at Lincoln High kept in contact with Bob after he moved to Fort Lee." Rita spent ten minutes providing details on the hunting lodge, the fall expedition, and the lodge gossip. Rita stopped talking as Vinnie faked a yawn.

Blanca asked, "And how is this connected?"

"I'm not sure. Bob Reinhardt's wife died from cancer and he raised his daughter alone, staying in their big house until her graduation two years ago. Glen figured Reinhardt wanted the stability for his daughter, which makes sense. Once the daughter graduated and went to college, Reinhardt bought a luxury Fort

Lee condo that reduced his New York commute. But Glen said the lodge gossip suggested this gave Reinhardt the freedom to have a host of different women stay overnight without prying suburbanite eyes. Reinhardt's reputation for being a ladies' man predated his wife's death, it seems."

Vinnie's fingers tapped rhythmically on his desktop like a piano keyboard. Rita had no intention to speed up her narrative. To get her facts in order without notes she mentally reviewed the evening activity, which required careful censoring.

"Turns out Bob's daughter was a cheerleader. 'Quite the babe' was the way Brett described her to Glen." Her voice rose saying Brett's name.

"Babe? Sounds tame given what he wrote about you on Facebook," said Vinnie.

Rita shrugged. She omitted Glen's opinion that no woman compared to her while fondling her breasts and his cock pressed at her wet labia. "Glen said the cheerleader's reputation made her a bitch."

"Now that's more of what I'd expect from Brett."

"No, not Brett. This was the school's faculty opinion, repeated by Emily to Glen. The girl boasted about being captain of the cheerleading squad and bullied other students, ridiculing them on social media. One girl's family moved home to get their daughter away from Bob's kid. Then, uh... this is upsetting, Ellen, the girl who left, she committed suicide, and it was allegedly connected to Bob Reinhardt's daughter who had continued to stalk her online. He heard the girl's parents asked Bob to stop his daughter, but he did nothing or very little to end it. But this is only rumor."

Vinnie gave a long whistle, but Blanca was up and marching out the door.

"Where you going?" Vinnie voice subdued, undemanding.

"That school," said Blanca, holding her nose, "*huele a mierda.* And I'm sure there's more *mierda* to uncover. I'm going to my computer to shovel."

Rita said to Vinnie, "I did good, didn't I?"

"Yeah, fuckin' unbelievable." Vinnie looked at his hand, not knowing the number of fingers to hold up.

Wrong Cell

Chapter 16

Blanca's hands rested over her stomach, as if in pain. She softly pronounced the suicide girl's name with barely moving lips, revealing the former Lincoln High student's identity. With head shaking, Blanca's voice rose. "This is too much. I want to run home and hold my kids. Protect them."

Pacing the room, Vinnie sputtered, "I know. Aside from suicide, which is the worst, there are other ways that bullies mess up kids. Depression, drug use as a type of self-medication, stress-induced mental illnesses, and family discord with accusatory finger pointing everywhere." He stopped.

Seconds past, each staring at some unimportant focal point until they looked at each other, tacitly agreeing that the investigation required an interview with the dead girl's parents. No one dared speak, afraid it would be taken as volunteering for the task. Blanca took the initiative, acknowledging that the need and the delicacy required a pair. She hastened to disqualify herself on the grounds she rarely did interviews, and as a mother of three her emotions were too volatile. Vinnie and Rita slumped, accepting that the task fell to them. Blanca touched Vinnie's arm. "I wish we had never taken Roger Bryant's retainer for this case."

***

Route 17 had light traffic for a Saturday morning. Vinnie wondered if shoppers had taken a day's rest. They arrived in northern Bergen County faster than planned. The "suicide parents," that awful but accurate appellative, shocked Blanca by granting an interview with Vinnie and Rita; the two investigators were equally shocked that they had not escaped the assignment.

A bright-eyed young boy opened the front door of a split-level home. He looked at Vinnie and Rita like they were exotic lost creatures arrived on his doorstep. "Mom, there are two strangers here," he called over his shoulder.

By strangers does he mean strange? Vinnie thought as he looked at the boy. *Would he remember his sister? What effect would his sister's suicide have on him in later life?*

A pleasant woman stood behind the child, plump but nothing outsized. She wore her role of typical suburban mother as if she was happy, living a normal life. She smiled, but without suggesting pleasure at seeing the two of them on her doorstep—more to acknowledge their existence.

"I thought our appointment was for ten am? Doesn't matter. I'm Marge Ritter. Please come in."

They followed Marge into the kitchen at the rear of the house. A sill extended the length of the countertop, and a large window overlooked the fenced backyard beyond. Vinnie touched Rita's shoulder, then pointed to a vase centered above the sink. Rita remarked to Marge on the beautiful flowers and was told they came from Fine Flowers, along with several outdoor plants and the magnificent entry pot, which neither Rita nor Vinnie had noticed.

At the table a man of average build held a coffee mug to his lips. "Bill, this is Rita and Vinnie. They're here to talk to us about Ellen." He did not shake hands, limiting his greeting to a mild grunt.

There was no real discussion until Vinnie had coffee and Rita herbal tea. As they finished their drinks over small talk the boy who had opened the door for Vinnie and Rita rushed into the room. Marge took hold of him as his arms wrapped around her waist. BJ, short for Bill Junior she explained, was eleven years old. He announced his plan to go next door to play with Jimmy. "Okay, sweetie. But if you and Jimmy go anywhere tell us first." The boy smiled, giving assurances he would, using the kitchen door to enter the backyard. Vinnie assumed there was a gate into Jimmy's yard.

"It was four years ago, but it feels like yesterday." Marge's voice was strong as the conversation moved from banality to the reason for the visit. With a steady pitch, she described their home, Bill's job as an electrician, and hers as a part-time secretary. "Ellen was a wonderful girl. A talented painter." Her pitch wavered, her voice less steady.

"She was our beautiful daughter, and now..." Bill interrupted his wife, his deep voice accenting his distress. He cracked his knuckles, words of disgust and recrimination aimed at no one, everyone, himself, his wife. By the time Ellen's parents finished they had unearthed their cavernous despair, an exercise Vinnie was sure Marge and Bill returned to frequently.

"Relentless. Online, goddam Facebook, Snapchat, Twitter, texting. The whole goddam connection thing. Ellen never stood a chance." Bill's eyebrows knitted together, adding force to his words. "Can you imagine being berated every waking moment of your day? It was like Ellen was a prisoner of war, except the Geneva Convention outlaws mental torture yet our kid had daily doses of it." He choked, putting his hand to his mouth. "She... she... was laying in her blood. She had taken so many pills to numb her pain as she slit her wrists, and not across but along the vein, like she had studied how to do it. No doubt using the fucking Internet to show her how. I found her on her bedroom floor, laying in blood, piss, and excrement all around. She was purple, her... uh... her mouth... uh... twisted and—" Bill stopped, his voice cracking. He inhaled deeply. "Her tongue was swollen, and she was clutching her childhood teddy... oh Christ she... she..." He broke into a full cry and Marge wept with him.

After a few minutes, Marge put her hand over her husband's. "When we found out about the bullying we were beside ourselves. Ellen didn't want to tell us. She was too embarrassed I imagine. That awful Jessica Reinhardt orchestrated a vendetta for no apparent reason." Ellen caught her breath. "We went to the school, and they promised to talk to her, but said their hands were tied."

"Goddam bullshit. I'd like to show them what it means to have your hands tied. I'd cut theirs off and stick them in their sanctimonious mouths." Bill banged the table with his fists, his voice harsh and his face flushed. "Our daughter's dead, and they sent us flowers with their condolences. Even had a goddam memorial service at the school... I... I..." He stopped, both hands balled into fists.

"We'll never have her back. Do you understand...? No, how could you." Marge paused, her head shaking. "How could anyone understand if they haven't experienced losing a child?" She whimpered cries and wiped her tears with a napkin. "Wait, I want to read from Ellen's diary." A few minutes passed in silence as they waited for Marge Ritter to return, clutching a brown notebook.

"'Ellen's a cuntasaurus, thick as pig shit,'" read Marge, "'so shouldn't be hard to keep her off the school Broadway trip.'" Marge recalled the first time she read this comment. "I wondered why Ellen didn't want to go. A school parent with theater connections got the class matinee tickets for *Hamilton*. We received a PTA notice about it, but Ellen said she wasn't interested. How many other events did she opt out of for fear of ridicule? Then there's this: 'A brown nose mud dove, thinks she'll get on the student council with her dumbass complaint campaign. Nobody votes for her or you'll be next.'"

Marge turned the pages. I think this posting is what pushed her. "'A mental retard who'd mess up her own suicide, the stupid cunt.'"

She looked up. "Ellen sent Facebook messages and tweets as public pleas for everyone to stop, but they fell on deaf ears. No one paid any attention to what it was doing to her."

"I'm so sorry," Vinnie said, his voice subdued, near cracking. This was his weakness, quick to empathize and even quicker to become emotional. He wanted to run out of the house. He had nothing else to say. Rita followed his lead, making no comment or asking questions. They waited in silence, but not for too long.

"We'll never be happy again. We hold it together for BJ, and that's the only reason we keep up this facade," said Marge, her voice flat, the emotion gone.

"I tell you," brayed Bill, "that guy Reinhardt got what he deserved. He did nothing to stop his daughter, even after we called him. We pleaded with him to intervene. Well, I'll tell you something, and I'll deny it if you repeat it, but if his daughter's head got blown off I won't shed a tear for her. She a wicked, evil bitch, a weapons-grade *cunt* that doesn't deserve to live."

Ten minutes later Vinnie and Rita exited with a simple thanks to the Ritters for sharing Ellen's story. Neither spoke in the car, as if Bill Ritter's heated acrimony had seared their ears. A gridlocked Route 17, with stop-start progress, had Vinnie break the silence, suggesting the traffic jam was an outcome of New Jersey residents awakening to find unspent money in their house, so they all rushed to one of Paramus's malls to relieve themselves of their burdensome tender. It wasn't funny, but it was enough levity to kick-start their conversation.

Vinnie assessed the interview and Rita agreed there was only one word for it—excruciating. Marge Ritter's nonstop lament, guilt, and anger; Bill Ritter lashing out at anyone associated with Lincoln High. Hearing Ellen's torturous diary read by her parents with the reverence of a Bible. And the foreshadowing of Ellen's suicide.

But the eye-opener came with Marge's appeal to a teacher to intervene. All her pleading, and the teacher voicing platitudes that Ellen would be okay, offering insipid excuses for not intervening. They knew who would be their next interview.

***

Work on other projects delayed Vinnie and Rita's return to northern Bergen County for several days. When they arrived at Lincoln High they negotiated the hallways to find the woman Marge Ritter cited as Ellen's complacent homeroom teacher.

"So, you knew?" asked Vinnie looking at the middle-aged woman.

The teacher nodded as if confirming the words to herself, her voice barely audible, "Yes. A tragedy what happened to that girl."

"Her name was *Ellen*!" Rita's stern face and piercing eyes emphasized the contempt in her near shout.

"Yes, Ellen." The teacher's voice stammered. "Who can be sure how things happen? How any individual might react?"

"You didn't think it preventable? Worth a try?" Rita's voice rumbled.

"Uh, well, uh, I mean, who can predict that kind of tragic outcome?"

"Lots of people. If not suicide then depression, loss of self-esteem, harm of one kind or another, over-reliance on alcohol or recreational drugs, maybe even hard drugs. Shall I go on?" Rita's voice jack-hammered at the teacher until Vinnie's hand gently touched her elbow.

"Why didn't you stop the girls, especially Jessica Reinhardt? Say something. File a school report."

"I did. I told the principal and the then vice principal for discipline, Mrs. Wasilewski, who said they weren't bad girls, just silly teenagers doing bad stuff who got carried away. Most had excellent academic credentials. Played on the girls' teams, hockey, soccer, and cheerleaders too. A few were in drama and performed in school plays. One was in the choir. Jessica was homecoming queen."

Vinnie's puckered lips produced clucks and gurgles. Rita's neck elongated.

"What could I do? It was a private matter. None of it happened on school computers."

With a snort Vinnie said, "How about putting a note in their school files referencing incidents of anti-social behavior? I'm sure colleges frown on students with questionable attitudes. Or expel them from team sports. There's plenty of ways to exert pressure on kids—and their parents."

The teacher looked outside where a strong wind moved the winter branches and debris over the school lawn. "You know, Jessica herself was vulnerable. She lost her mother to cancer just before her freshman year. A real blow. Her father raised her but he couldn't handle it very well. We had to consider Jessica's well-being too."

Her words incited Vinnie, he sputtered, spittle flew from his lips, and his venom was aimed squarely at the teacher. "Even if you believe that BS excused Jessica's actions, it does not for you or your colleagues. You are the adults. You have a responsibility to protect all students, whether they are A-students, athletes, or fu... fudgin' outcasts." Vinnie's face flushed, his breath shallow.

"Vinnie, it's okay." Rita rubbed Vinnie's back, then turned to the teacher. "What about Jessica's mother?"

"Lorraine Reinhardt. I thought you knew. She was head of the English department at Monroe High School but before her promotion she taught English here at Lincoln. Everyone liked Lorraine. A beautiful woman. You could see where Jessica gets her good looks from. Her death was a real blow. Every teacher attended her funeral, a lot of the students too."

A quick glance from Vinnie to Rita showed their simultaneous enlightenment.

"Did you know her well?" asked Rita.

"Just barely. She left for Monroe the year I arrived, but I heard so much about her. Even in a single term I liked her. A wonderful person. What a shame."

"More than Ellen's suicide... you fu—" An arm took hold of Vinnie's, pulling him up.

"Let's go. I think we've learned what we needed."

There were no words of thanks as Vinnie and Rita exited the classroom. Vinnie turned to Rita in the hallway. "I think we have our motive. Someone is as disgusted as us and is acting on it. We must find out precisely how Lincoln High handles bullying."

Neither wanted to say Bill Ritter's name but neither could forget the anger over his daughter's suicide—he would be high on any suspect murder list. They both wanted to deny this fact but couldn't.

Chapter 17

Under the guise of parents moving into town, Vinnie and Blanca entered the high school office. Their professed reason was to learn about the standards of education in the neighborhood before purchasing an overpriced one-point-two-million home. Blanca was Vinnie's wife in this scenario, holding his hand. She made an exception to her refusal to do interviews policy because neither Vinnie's nor Rita's acting ability could fake a loving couple. Besides, Blanca was the only one of the three with school interview experience, with two sons in elementary school and a daughter in pre-school. She knew the drill, the buzzwords, and had the school bullshit detector.

Entering the main corridor, Vinnie searched for Brett Dingle. Blanca reminded him tartly that the late afternoon appointment with vice principal Judith McArthur coincided with football practice. "So?" grunted Vinnie then smiled.

"What now?" Blanca's face was stern.

"We're the perfect married couple if you keep up the nagging, sweetheart."

"Sure, honey. And by the way, can Ethel and I sing in the band tonight?" Blanca pouted. "You know Desi Arnaz was Cuban and I'm Puerto Rican, right? Or you think we're all the same?" She had objected to his choice of famous characters for them, unlike his choice for Rita, the talented Puerto Rican Rita Moreno.

"Always a wiseass," answered Vinnie.

"*Besas mi trasero.*"

"Do you kiss your children with that mouth?" Blanca let Vinnie have the last word.

They entered the vice principal's office still holding hands, Vinnie's knuckles white from Blanca's squeeze. "Pleased to meet you, Mr. and Mrs. Ricardo." Vice principal McArthur was a tall, somewhat plump woman in her early fifties.

Vinnie provided the invented backstory, a ramble about moving from Garden City, Long Island, reducing Vinnie's commute to his Saddle River job.

Blanca's face narrowed, stifling a yawn. "We're looking into schools before purchasing. Our children's education is obviously important to us."

"Of course," said the vice principal in her sympathetic administrator tone.

She couldn't care less about our children. She's a liar, thought Vinnie, overlooking the false pretense of the visit.

Blanca continued to gently question Mrs. McArthur on her experience at Lincoln High School. Vinnie had warned her: "Don't be too direct or impatient or we'll put her on the defensive." So Blanca waited.

Mrs. McArthur explained that she replaced Mrs. Wasilewski after she became principal at a private girls' high school. Before either became administrators they both taught English at Lincoln High. Blanca thought it time to ask about the bullying policy. She used the guise that their imaginary child's former school was too laissez-faire in their attitude and that this concerned her.

The vice principal said nothing while Vinnie fidgeted. *Yeah, don't step into it. I'll bet you do laissez-faire if the price is right.*

"What about here, at Lincoln, Mrs. McArthur? How is bullying handled?" Blanca asked.

With eyelids blinking and a tiger's grin, the vice principal leaned back, hands clasped. "We have a strict zero-tolerance policy."

The typical party line, thought Vinnie. He coughed, gave a gritty smile, and rested his elbows on his knees. "Is that also true for social media? Texting?"

"Monitoring online and cell phone activity outside school is unlawful. We can't invade students' privacy."

"Sure," jumped in Blanca, preempting Vinnie, whose hands tugged at his pants. "But if a student or parent complains, you know, identifies online bullying, then what?"

"We do what we can, but legalities restrict our options."

Again the hiding behind legal excuses. Vinnie's voice became strident. "So do nothing, let a student suffer?" Vinnie squawked, accusatory, and Mrs. McArthur leaned forward, placing her hands on the desktop. Her tone matched Vinnie's, suggesting that Mr. and Mrs. Ricardo should address bullying questions to the disciplinary dean.

"Wasn't that your position before becoming vice principal?" Vinnie pointed his index finger at her.

Mrs. McArthur stood. "I don't know what you want, but I don't think you're interested in our curriculum. I think you should leave." She walked to the door and held it open. "Thank you for stopping by. If you have further questions, please contact the principal."

In the corridor, Blanca took Vinnie's hand. "Wait."

A secretary came out the office door. She acted surprised to see Blanca and Vinnie standing in the hall.

"I hope we didn't keep you too long?" said Blanca, sounding merry.

"That's okay. Sometimes prospective parents stay long after school closes. We never leave the principal or vice principal with people we don't know... oh, gosh, that sounds awful!"

"Not at all," replied Blanca with her new version of cheerful. "Can we walk you to your car? It's getting dark."

"Not necessary."

"We're in no hurry." Vinnie reintroduced himself and Blanca.

The secretary nodded, saying she remembered. "Mr. and Mrs. Ricardo, right? I'm Doris, like Doris Day." Vinnie thought he caught a wink. He expected her to burst into a chorus of "Que Sera, Sera."

As they walked Doris revealed she had been the school secretary for twenty-four years with retirement looming in twelve months.

"Schools are difficult these days, aren't they?" Blanca's words were spoken with a quiet reverence.

The secretary nodded. "Remember the days without social media, cell phones, texting? The world's not the same, that's for sure."

By the time they reached the parking lot, Vinnie and Blanca had learned about the prior vice principal, Mrs. Wasilewski. Doris caller her "a good woman," but implied she was not a good fit for the public high school in today's age of Internet and kids knowing and seeing more than they should. Doris thought her former boss was better off moving to a private all-girls' school.

"Why?" asked Blanca.

"Discipline's easier at a private school. They expel the unruly, but that's not really a public school option."

With her hands clasped together and a nod, Blanca agreed with Doris's wise words.

Vinnie stopped walking. "So, vice principal McArthur's more capable?"

As she was a few steps ahead of Vinnie, Doris stopped to turn, her laughing sounding like a steam valve releasing pressure. "She thinks she is but anyone can bury their head in the sand, bending over for parents with money and influence." The secretary covered her mouth. "Oh, I shouldn't have said that. It's been a difficult day and I'm really tired."

"That's okay, we won't repeat it." Vinnie turned to Blanca, each nodding to the other. Vinnie warmed to Doris.

As if being cautious, Doris spoke in a subdued voice, confirming Mrs. McArthur's involvement with the disciplinary case of the boy beaten up by the football players. Blanca moved closer, suggesting a confidentiality between them. Doris lowered her voice, revealing secrets that normally stay locked inside the administrative and faculty lounge.

"It wasn't the entire team, just two boys. One is no longer here and the other boy isn't all bad, just easily led astray. Mrs. McArthur knew they bullied others but... well, I shouldn't really be telling you this."

"I understand," said Blanca, hand to her heart. "You see, our boy was bullied too, so this is important to me—to us. He suffered physical and emotional injury. Do you have children?"

"Yes, three grown boys. Thank God they never had to experience it." Doris looked over her shoulder toward the school and expressed her not-so-disguised disapproval of Mrs. McArthur's handling of bullies when she was disciplinary dean. "She tried pretty hard to ignore what was going on, when it was really quite obvious."

"Really? What happened?" Blanca's voice rose.

"Swept under the rug." After a short pause, Doris explained that the two football boys' parents made a sizable payoff. "The victim received a big settlement. His parents won't have to worry about college tuition, I can tell you that."

Blanca probed, saying that she worried about the long-term effect of bullying on her son. Doris agreed, having seen the impact on a friend's daughter, and also her brother's sister-in-law's son. While other bullying disciplinary events happened at Lincoln, only the one involved a serious violent physical attack. Everyone knew the football players pushed kids around, into lockers, punched arms, that kind of stuff but nothing that caused any real physical harm. Vinnie was about to reply but Blanca took his arm.

Taking control of his emotions, Vinnie pushed Doris harder, asking her to share more, promising the conversation was confidential. As they reached the parking lot Doris started by reciting qualifiers to her comments, but before she reached any substance a white delivery van drove up, the driver's window open.

"Hi, Doris. I got held up by traffic. Accident on Route 9."

"Oh, that's okay, Greg. We can go over the arrangements tomorrow. It's been a busy day."

"You sure? I'm really sorry I wasted your time."

"Please, Greg, no need to apologize."

As the van headed off, Doris turned to face Blanca and Vinnie. "Greg Fine does the flower arrangements for big events. A wonderful man. Such a shame what happened to—" The van stopped and began to back up, interrupting the secretary.

"Doris, I nearly forgot." The driver's door swung open, and out stepped a man that could lift mature trees. He opened the side panel door, ducked inside, and reappeared with a sing-song "Happy birthday to you, Doris." He held up a large vase containing a dozen yellow roses and a single white in the center.

"Oh, Greg, they're beautiful! Thank you." Greg performed a small bow and carried the flowers over to Doris's car.

***

Vinnie should have brought Blanca to Penn Station, let her take the LIRR to Garden City. No, he insisted on driving, and was now delayed in LIE traffic—the Long Island Expressway parking lot being a better descriptor. He finally returned to his condo after eight pm.

Ben greeted Vinnie, extending a glass of red wine, while he stood in his tanning briefs and nothing else. Vinnie's supper was on reheat.

"I take it you have something special for dessert." Vinnie touched Ben's low-hung pouch, stretching the fabric.

"Could be."

"Do you want to hear about—"

"Do I look like I want to hear?" Ben spread his legs, arms held overhead, nothing but bare skin except for the skimpy trunks taut around his loin.

"I need to call Dan to set up tomorrow's meeting. I tried while driving back but got no answer."

"You know why? He and Ginny are having their 'special dessert.' Did you leave a message?"

Vinnie nodded while chewing.

137

"Then hurry. Your dessert's going soft."

***

Vinnie fell into a deep sleep minutes after "dessert," exhausted from the long, emotional day. Two hours later he awoke, viewing Ben spreadeagled naked on his stomach, his mountainous ass blocking Vinnie's view of the night table clock. Vinnie considered a remount, but weariness lingered even though sleep now felt impossible. He shuffled to his study, jotting thoughts into his computer program.

- Learn about Mrs. Wasilewski (R?)
- Talk to parents of kid bullied by Brett and Ken (V and R)
- Investigate more teenage suicides throughout Bergen County (B and D)
- Discover next victim? (??)
- Who is Greg Fine and Fine Flowers?

Vinnie read the list and deleted the last bullet. It was extra work for no reason.

He thought of Ben's bulbous ass and riding atop him pretending to be at a rodeo. He chuckled at his thoughts: a commando act on Ben, an ass-in-action. His somnambulant haze cleared, and his mood darkened. He typed one more bullet.

- Ass-in-action —>Assassination.

Reading the last bullet, he deleted it. Yet one thought dominated: *It's not over yet. Something fuckin' bad is going to happen.*

Chapter 18

"What's up? Why the eight am meeting? I have kids to get to school. Al isn't too happy, me running out before breakfast." Blanca placed her coffee mug and bagel on Vinnie's desk as she moved her chair closer to his. The coffee aroma seeped up Vinnie's nostrils, recalling his disturbed night and dark thoughts.

With arms crossed behind her back, Rita followed Blanca into Vinnie's office. "I rushed from my morning class. I had no time to cool down. How long will this take? My next class is at eleven but I need to set up." Rita lifted one leg on the chair and touched her nose to her kneecap, then repeated with the other leg.

Vinnie did not look up from his computer screen. "We need additional qualifiers and data, only we work backward. That's what Dan said."

"You talked to Dan? When? Don't you respect anyone's morning?" Blanca turned the computer to face her. Rita crouched behind Blanca.

Vinnie tapped the monitor with his index finger, where a copy of his notes from last night filled the screen. "Dan says we could add rows by looking for bullying reports not linked to suicides. Check news articles and human-interest stories on bullying."

Rita dragged a chair across between Blanca's and Vinnie's. She leaned forward, her elbows resting on her thighs, her fists supporting her chin. "I thought I saw Dan leave UltraFit when I arrived. Does he get up at five?" She bent backwards, cracking her spine.

Vinnie closed his eyes.

Blanca shuffled papers. She turned from Rita to Vinnie. "And why exactly would we do this? More to the point, how?" Blanca rubbed her eyes, picking up her coffee from the edge of Vinnie's desk. "And did I mention why?"

Vinnie leaned back, hands clasped behind his head, a know-it-all pose, then placed his fingers on the keyboard and mouse. He used the on-screen cursor to highlight "Discover next victim." "It happened last night, while I was thinking with Ben."

Rita and Blanca groaned.

Yup, skip the details. "It's relevant, I swear." He lifted his right hand, palm out, as if taking an oath.

After a few minutes of impossible-to-follow metaphors and analogies it was clear he was only spreading confusion rather than enlightenment. Blanca broke Vinnie's ramble. "Get to the point." She slumped in her seat while Rita performed calf extensions.

With a rat-a-tat of double entendre sentences he coughed out words until a reference to "Ben's mountainous ass" slipped out. Blanca's chair screeched along the tile surface as she pushed back to walk out. Rita followed.

"No, come back, I can explain." Vinnie ran after the women. He reached Blanca, tugging at her arm. She stood on her toes, her index finger under his nose. "Spit it out in one word."

"Assassination."

Blanca dropped her hand, her facial expression blank.

Rita leaned on the doorjamb. "Which means what? Remember, I'm a novice."

His hand moving as if directing traffic, Vinnie guided the women back into his office. "If I'm right, more lives are at risk."

"Who? Why?" Blanca's words cut like a razor. She pushed her near-empty coffee mug around the desktop.

"Weren't you listening? It's a feeling. What's with you and facts?" Vinnie's lips curled.

Arms up, Blanca turned to Rita, her head angling to Vinnie. "A fool. *Chorra. El burro sabe mas que él.* Not even donkey smart."

Vinnie gave Blanca the middle finger.

He asked the women to scour the Internet for school bullying discussions. Search online newspapers, social media like Instagram, Facebook, Twitter, and non-standard sources. Look across districts and even outside Bergen County for new data, additional schools, more incidences. He and Rita would attend a few school sporting events, try to coax gossip from students and parents about the problem.

***

The BIG team spent an entire week gathering data until Vinnie was ready to call Dan.

"Twelve? That's an incredible number." Dan's joyous delight was clear on Vinnie's Bluetooth headset.

"Yeah," said Vinnie. "And that covers two years. Blanca conjures online information and pulls rabbits from hats. She pressured a reporter friend for his bullying research, the stuff that didn't make it to press."

Dan apologized in advance, but to enter and analyze the data he needed more time. Vinnie waited an anxious several hours. His cell finally rang after ten pm, Dan's name flashing on caller ID.

"Anything?" Vinnie spoke like he'd not heard from Dan in years.

"There's a pattern. Nothing definitive, but a correlation. Remember that our information is subjective, so very soft. Parent anger is not quantifiable. This could all be artifact. You'll need legs on the ground to create actual links."

Vinnie called Rita. She complained about the late hour, telling him she was in a difficult yoga position. A shout came over the line. "How long do I need to fucking stay like this?" The man's voice sounded like an X-room young buck Vinnie knew—as Ben's spouse, Vinnie met most of the X-room members.

"We need another round of interviews, which may be tricky. Come in early tomorrow. Oh, and untwist Daryl. Doesn't he compete in a month?"

***

Arranging parent interviews of bullied students felt like running a marathon without wearing shoes. Phone numbers were not easily obtained as most were unlisted. They expected none of the parents would agree to rehash the awful physical and psychological violence perpetrated against their children. They might even perceive the interviews themselves to be bullying. Among the twelve families contacted came unanticipated surprise: two families agreed to Blanca's request to meet Vinnie and Rita under two non-negotiable conditions: no children would be present and anonymity would be guaranteed.

The interviews produced nothing new, not at the start. Vinnie had deduced most of the information from common sense and knowledge of society. The parents corroborated his assumption: capricious teenage whims more than rational criteria selected their children to suffer cruel, vituperative abuse. A new portrayal about bullying was revealed as the parents retold stories from their lawyers on other bullying cases. The information vague, non-specific to avoid jeopardizing attorney–client privilege. Here too, Vinnie correctly surmised the outcome before hearing the conclusion: bullied kids in middle and upper-income communities received substantial monetary compensation, while kids in lower-income communities received small sums or nothing. For rich communities, settlement amounts could reach six figures. Of course, in the severest cases with terrible injuries, bullies were expelled or sent to juvenile detention—but never for rich kids. As Vinnie guessed.

The information had been anticipated until the parents revealed their children were under psychiatric care for post-traumatic stress disorder. One child continued with therapy to help with lingering thoughts of suicide. Each parent faulted the school administration. What shocked Vinnie and Rita most was the intense anger directed at the bully's parents rather than the bully.

At the BIG review, Vinnie said what everyone thought. "This is worse than I imagined. I mean I was bullied for being gay but I had support from classmates and teachers. But this is... I don't know what it is."

"Well, I do." Rita was twisting, her voice knife-edge sharp. "I'd like to—"

"Okay. Let's not go there." Blanca tapped her pen on a pad of paper. "What next?"

With his head drooping, Vinnie's voice was barely audible. "We need more insight into the bullies' parents. We have a good picture of the bullied kids and those doing it." He stopped. "We only know two living families that fall into the extreme category. Roger Bryant's our client, so he's out. That leaves Glen Dingle."

The room's overhead neon lights hummed in the silence that stretched out.

"It will have to be Rita." Vinnie rested his chin on his chest as he announced his decision.

"What? You said no further contact." Rita walked to the doorway and then back to Vinnie's desk.

"I know what I said, but I don't see another way. Can you act professional, with no—" Vinnie formed a fist, pumping his forearm to and fro.

"How dare you!" Rita leaned back, her words sputtering, neck taut, and eyebrows marching upward to her hairline.

"Stop now. What's wrong with you two?" Blanca walked out the door and turned before closing it. "Stop acting like children. I'm sick of this immature behavior."

After fifteen minutes Rita came out of Vinnie's office. "I'm sorry, I overreacted." Blanca accepted Rita's apology, and a moment later Vinnie approached her. He took Blanca in his arms and hugged her tight. "Me too. Like you said many times, I'm a big *pendejo*." He tapped his ass. "Enormous dick too."

Blanca's open palm tapped Vinnie's cheek. "You really are like a teenager." She hugged him back. "Okay, boys and girls, let's get going. Mommy forgives you and for your penance say five Hail Marys and no sex tonight."

Ten minutes later, Rita got ready to leave for the day. "I'm seeing Glen tomorrow for dinner. I remember, Hail Marys and no sex tonight. See ya." With a big grin and an exaggerated arm swinging Rita left the office.

Vinnie faked a goodbye wave, then said to Blanca, "Wait. Does she mean no sex tonight, postponing it until tomorrow? That deceptive lying—" Blanca's slap was hard. "Ouch! *Hey!* Fu..."

Blanca raised her hand again.

"Okay, okay, I'll wait and see," Vinnie said, rubbing at his raw cheek.

Chapter 19

Rita cradled the phone, moving her tongue as she waited. On the third ring he answered the call transferred by his secretary to his office line. She stuttered hearing his voice.

"Oh, Rita. So glad you called. I tried to reach—"

Before he finished, Rita stopped him. She didn't bother with excuses, but launched into her wishing to see him again. His chuckle reassured her. "Me too." She thought he sounded like a nervous boy, and wondered what she seemed to him.

"Come for dinner. I'll cook and plan to stay this time."

Risky. Would she meet Brett? She countered his offer with a night at a five-star Meadowlands hotel. Glen laughed. He said he knew why. She was shy about his teenage son, which was clear when she declined to stay their first night together.

"I understand. It takes time to get use to teenagers," he said with a hearty laugh. Rita did not join in, but he did not see her frown on the other end of call.

He assured her that Brett had plans for an overnighter with his teammates. He laughed again, saying the home-cooked meal had another advantage but stopped himself. Rita completed his thought: the bedroom was a shorter distance from the table than a restaurant to a hotel room. Their laughs melded.

'Plan carefully had been Vinnie's advice. Rita reviewed the points to cover on the drive to Mahwah. Vinnie suggested a stealth approach to the interview: let the conversation evolve and flow. As part of this low-profile concept, she parked her car in front of a nearby house, making her visit less noticeable to nosy neighbors.

Standing at Glen's front door, she turned. Her car was out of sight. How would Glen interpret this? Was it a mistake not parking in his garage like the first time? Should she retrieve her car and park in the driveway? The front door opened before she rang the doorbell, the decision made.

Rita pushed Glen back from the threshold, dropping a large bag on the floor. Glen bent to peck her cheek and she put a pipe-wrench grip around his neck and steadied his head as she vacuum-sealed their lips. Her tongue-thrashing kiss surprised herself as much as Glen.

In their embrace, Rita lifted her back foot to push the door shut behind her, as if remembering this was a stealth operation, but it was an action that nearly toppled them and broke the kiss. Glen didn't let loose and spoke in a somber voice, soaked in despair, describing his search for her, her non-functioning phone, and no fitness website.

The BIG investigators knew Glen would question his inability to contact Rita. They sought a three-S rationalization: simple, surefire, self-explanatory. The non-working phone number was because Rita stupidly mixed old and new business cards. The IT geeks had taken down all traces of her original fitness website while preparing a new design.

Rita looked into Glen's eyes, a few inches from her face, his lips opening in a smile. Did he buy her explanations? She stuttered, trying to improvise more detail until stopped by Glen's finger on her lips. "Doesn't matter. You called, and that's what counts. I can't tell you how happy I am that you are here." He inhaled as if preventing a sob.

The heat of his body radiated outward, engulfing her. She wanted him to set her on fire, immolate the memories of her ex-boyfriend. She tugged Glen's hair, pulled his head back, and kissed him until his lungs collapsed.

"Woooooow," Glen's words gushed.

Bending to her bag beside her, Rita retrieved a bow-wrapped package. "This is for you."

"Rita, you didn't need to bring me a gift."

"I think I did. Open it."

"Let's have a drink first. Red or white?"

Both laughed while Glen opened his gift. He examined each label in turn on the three bottles containing the sex lubricant. "I like the Honeysuckle Delight for the extra stimulation. Look underneath the bottle."

Glen pulled out a set of six condoms labeled "ultra-thin." Rita thought his smile might break his jaw. "Put supper on hold?" Her controlled laugh hid her anxiety—this was not in Vinnie's plan; it was out of sequence even for Rita's hidden agenda.

The bedroom felt familiar, much like Glen. Together they chose a lubricant to match the condom, which Glen said was like nothing he had ever used before. He quickly added that he and Emily had stopped using condoms, at first to conceive Brett, then... he tailed off mid-sentence, a sheepish smile on his face. But he no longer swallowed hard on saying Emily's name like he did at the restaurant.

She heard glee in Glen guessing her calls. He managed to get "Dove Fuck" on her D-F shout. He was chuckling as her legs hung over his shoulders, herself upside down stroking his sheathed erection and applying more lubricant.

The sex was better than the first time. Rita relaxed. She had a plan; not the investigation plan, but the one to meet her needs and it worked.

They enjoyed the intimacy. Rita had multiple climaxes and Glen rose three times. Rita laughed away his apology over his weak third performance. Another shared laugh.

They devoured the main course around nine. The wine blew Rita's diet so she compensated with a minuscule portion of potato au gratin. To please Rita, Glen prepared a fish dish. Rita complemented him on his cooking skills.

"Just so you know, the pie's from a bakery. I couldn't do it all."

"Just a sliver and no ice cream please." Rita tapped her stomach.

Placing Rita's dessert plate in front of her, Glen tutted from behind, pinching her side. "Ooh, so fat." His head dropped over her shoulder and he kissed her cheek. "You are beautiful."

Rita's smile prevented her reply. She had never lacked for compliments, but unlike the others, Glen's were not banal about her strength or enhanced physical condition or acrobatic skill. He had none of the ex-boyfriend inanities: "Your tits are so hard." "I could eat your perfect ass." "I'm going to fucking pound your hard muscles."

Glen's words differed. He worshipped her as a woman and not just her body, even as he praised her physique. He tuned his tongue to her lips. To him her green eyes made all other greens appear gray. He licked at her nipples like they were syrup peaches. He would have held her until the dawn.

He stood behind her, skimming his fingers to tingle her arms.

"After this," poking her pie with her dessert fork, "we'll have seconds there?" She lifted her fork to point to the bedroom. "Compare products for our Amazon review?" Her hand motioned as if squeezing a tube.

Glen's eyebrows rose, his lips spread, and his hand tapped at his breast. Their joy-soaked laughter so loud it covered the noise of the front door opening. They stopped abruptly on hearing the words, "Hi, Dad."

Glen moved to the dining room archway, peering into the hallway.

Clumped there were four teenagers ranging from six foot to six-five, each with a Lincoln High leather football jacket and numbers pressed on their sleeves.

"Hi, Mr. Dingle," chorused the troop.

"Hey Dad, Doug's mother wasn't feeling too good so we went out for pizza. S'okay if the guys stay here tonight? The game's on and it might run late." Brett waved his friends to his room.

"Sure, that's fine—go ahead, boys. And if you're hungry, there's food in the fridge. I think you guys know where we keep the snacks, right?" Glen pointed to a side table, "Car keys here please. You can get them from me in the morning. Not that you would be drinking beer, right?" He tossed his head from side to side. The boys laughed. "Beer, Mr. Dingle?" said the largest. "What's that?"

"Smartass. Just don't overdo it. Keys, now."

As the group moved like cattle Glen called out, "Brett, wait. Let me introduce you to a friend."

Rita's spine stiffened, her back toward the hallway. Glen's body had blocked the view of her at the dining room table. Rita did not turn, instead her fork hung motionless over her pie. She whispered, "Maybe later," but Brett was already in the room.

At the table, Brett's arm outstretched, his palm open. In the instant he looked up from his hand to Rita's face, his hand reshaped into a pointing finger, his lips puckered like he was sucking a lemon. "What the fuck is *she* doing here?"

In two steps Glen's hands were on his son's shoulders. "How dare you speak like that to my friend? What the hell's wrong with you?"

"You don't know? Really? This is the bitch that came here a few weeks ago with her detective partner to talk to me about that thing at school with the Dellarosa kid and Ken."

In a split second, Glen's hand unfurled from Brett's jacket as he faced Rita.

"I can explain," she said, getting up from the table.

"It's true!" Glen folded, his hand on his stomach.

"I told you. This fucking cunt is stirring up trouble again." Brett's voice rose at takeoff speed, his anger a war cry.

With lightning-fast reaction, Glen slapped his son's face, a red mark imprinted on his cheek. The force propelled Brett backward, pushing him against a chair and knocking him to one knee. "Get out! Don't ever speak like that again in this house. Ever!" Glen screamed, his voice uncontrolled, his legs unsteady, one hand braced against the wall.

Brett's eyes filled with tears. The teammates assembled in the room, but no one spoke.

Glen looked at them, his voice calm yet stern. "Leave. All of you. You too, Brett." Glen's voice dropped, nearly inaudible. "Stay anywhere you like, I don't care. Sleep in your goddam car. Just get out." Glen was pointing to the front door, face sunburnt red, lips contorted, eyes squinting. Violence shook his body, then his eyes clouded, moisture filling the lower lids.

Not one boy spoke. Brett wiped his cheek with the back of his hand and sobbed once. His eyes penetrated Rita's as if he would tear her apart from the inside out. He followed his embarrassed friends, turned back, stared at his father, then slammed the front door to leave the room in mausoleum silence.

Glen sat down shakily, elbows on the table, hands covering his face. He spoke through his fingers. "I liked you. I thought I might even love you."

Rita cried. "Please, Glen, I can explain—"

"Explain? What's to explain? You used me. You don't care about me, I'm just a way to get at my son. Hasn't my life been destroyed enough? How could you be so cruel?" Glen stopped, and his body shuddered. Tears salted his cheeks. "Just when I thought I might have a life after Emily... look what you've done. My son will never speak to me again."

"No, that's not true." Rita moved to Glen's side, her hand touching his arm. He pushed it away like he was discarding a used paper cup.

"I have never hit Brett. Never. Not once in all his life. I... I..." Glen's sobbing increased. "Leave. Just go."

"Glen, please. Can't we talk about this? I didn't come to expose your son and bring up—"

Removing his hands from his face, Glen stared at Rita's twisting body, her eyes wide and pleading. His words were staunch, overcoming his emotion. "Then what? What do you want?"

"To find out about Emily's murder. Vinnie and I think there is a connection between her murder and the bullying."

"So, it is about that incident." He was beginning to shout as anger creased his face.

"No, not exactly."

Their words jumbled, neither listening to the other. Each spewing out, Glen's words an ensemble of anguish, anger, and accusation. Rita cried, unable to withstand the verbal battering. Eventually Glen sat slumped in his chair, repeating his demand for Rita to leave.

She walked away, defeated yet knowing Glen was no victor. At the door she turned once more to speak but heard Glen's shout. "I never want to see you again! If you or your partner come near my son, I will sue the hell out of you. Now get out!"

"Please—"

"For fuck's sake, do me this courtesy. I can't take any more pain." Glen covered his face, and Rita wished she had parked closer. She wanted to drive away fast, considered the possibilities of a fatal accident—anything to make amends for her transgression. Her chest tightened and she realized she was in love with Glen.

What to do with her life now?

Chapter 20

The spreadsheet's columns and rows married victim to victimizer. Dan concentrated, his blue pupils floating on glistening white sclera. His formula uncoiled the skein of data, and his mind peeled the psychological from the abstract. If this were purely theoretical, it would have been enjoyable.

"So," Vinnie said, hands slicking the sides of his head as if applying hair gel, "got any ideas?"

Hearing Dan's muttering was Vinnie's cue to leave, his talk an irritation. He returned two hours later, calling to Dan with one leg outside the door's threshold, "Anything?"

Dan's brow knitted. "We need more on this outlier."

"What fuckin' outlier?!" Vinnie's voice was extra high-pitched as he complained about Dan's obscurity.

"Again with the F-word."

"Really?" Vinnie rolled his eyes. "Okay, what fudgin' outlier?"

"The Bob Reinhardt outlier, remember?"

Vinnie shrugged.

"Have you checked family, friends, colleagues?"

Throwing his hands in the air as if he was seeking mercy, Vinnie said, "No, I've been sitting on my fuckin' ass doing nothing."

Dan shook his head. Vinnie was in full swing. "Okay, I fudgin' checked. Satisfied?"

A smile crossed Dan's face. "Yes on the marginal language improvement, and no on Reinhardt. You discovered nothing?"

"We dismissed Reinhardt as not relevant, remember?"

"Not anymore."

***

Vinnie entered the BIG office with his morning greeting when Blanca blocked him, tugged his sleeve, and pulled him into the hallway.

"Blanca, what are you doing?" Vinnie looked down at her frowning forehead. "Let go," he said as he struggled to loosen her grip.

"This is a preemptive intervention." Blanca's voice was hard.

"What? Have you gone mad? *Loco?*"

"Don't start with your pretend Spanish cursing."

Vinnie shrugged.

"She's not in a good place."

"Who?"

"Rita. You really are an idiot, Vinnie."

"What? Blanca, what's going on?"

After a poke in his shoulder, Vinnie moved against the wall but Blanca kept hold of his sleeve. She told him Rita was emotionally over the edge, arrived at BIG a mess: red eyed, puffy faced, and spoke no more than two sentences before going into Vinnie's office and shutting the door.

"Here's the clincher," said Blanca looking around conspiratorially. "Ben called, said Rita missed her dance exercise class without cancelling."

Vinnie whistled, raising his pitch an octave. "Oh my, a disaster." His voice lowered to a chortle. "Makes Hurricane Katrina look like a paper fan. Do you know how many classes I cut in college? Really! So she missed a class."

Blanca moved closer, her head tilted so far back Vinnie could see her tonsils move as she spoke. "*Verga*. Listen carefully. Rita has never, not ever missed a class. And she's in your office and not in her tight-ass leotard workout outfits. She looks like shit, which for her means something terrible has happened. She won't talk to me."

"Jesus. Should I go away?"

"How stupid can you get? Obviously she needs to talk to someone, and she wants it to be you."

"Me? That can't be right. We tried to patch things up, but we're superficial and bad liars, as you frequently point out."

Blanca released Vinnie's sleeve and pointed to the office. "Get in there now. I'll guide you. Watch me before you say anything."

They crossed the room and Vinnie gingerly opened the door to his office. Rita did not turn, remaining slumped in her seat like a discarded rag doll.

"Hey Rita. How's it going—" Vinnie felt Blanca's elbow in his side. He moved behind his desk, stopped by Blanca, who guided him to a straight-back chair pulled next to Rita's. Blanca moved another chair to Rita's other side, yet in foot-striking distance of Vinnie.

"I have news," said Rita in a monotone.

"Good."

"No, not good."

"I don't mean the news, I mean that you..." Vinnie stopped as Blanca waved a finger.

"I screwed up. Bad. Real bad. In fact I totally fucked up. I'm so sorry. I'm quitting, resigning, whatever. Don't pay me either, because I don't deserve it. I don't deserve anything."

Vinnie's mouth opened, his lips parted to grunt a reply.

"What?" Rita leaned forward.

"No."

"No? No, what?"

"No, you're not quitting, resigning, leaving, going away, and you are fuckin' going to continue working with Blanca and me at BIG."

"Didn't you hear me? I screwed things up for... well, for everyone. I've lost him." Rita burst into tears, sobbing, hands covering her face. Blanca motioned Vinnie to leave.

After a half-hour Vinnie returned, but Blanca waved him away again. This time he waited an hour.

"Can I come in?" he eventually asked at the door.

"Yes. Rita's gone."

"Gone? Gone how? Gone where?"

"Home to rest. She'll be back this afternoon."

"She okay?"

"What? You think I'm a super therapist? 'Blanca Santos cures psychological problems in an hour or your money back.' No, Rita won't be okay for a long time."

Vinnie listened to Blanca recount Rita's story. He cursed her duplicity and stupidity but also empathized. He knew about rejection, the abandonment of a person you hoped would be your life partner. For Rita it had happened twice in as many months.

"She needs therapy. We'll get Ben to help persuade her. But now let's focus on the case." Blanca nudged Vinnie from the computer to take command of the keyboard and she quickly typed a summary.

"I'll check details with Rita. Meanwhile, you update her for the next part. It won't be easy for her."

***

"We're going to follow up on Reinhardt." Vinnie sat hands folded, eyes straight at Rita, his voice flat. She seemed less cartoonish, her face not as long, but still not in her usual gym leotard.

"He's dead. What's to follow up on?"

"The daughter."

"Why? Hurt someone else?"

Vinnie's eyes swept his desktop.

"Don't you care about hurting people?" Rita's voice was strident.

"Yes, yes I do. Remember, I'm responsible for at least three people's deaths." A long silence followed. "And more people will die because someone's on a mission."

"Why one person and not two or three?"

"A hunch."

Rita scoffed. "Like I had a hunch Glen liked me?"

"Rita, it's not the same. And Glen did like you. He might even come round."

"I doubt it. I damaged his relationship with his son and that's on me."

While Rita wiped her eyes Vinnie looked away, his voice subdued. "It's only one person. I feel it. I need your help. Blanca can't take time away from her family for a trip to Chicago."

"Chicago?"

"That's where the parents of Karen Costermann live."

"Costermann?"

"Another girl Jessica Reinhardt taunted."

She recalled Glen mentioned the Costermann name. "And what's so important about the daughter?"

"Karen Costermann committed suicide."

"When's the flight?" Rita walked out of the office in long strides.

***

"So, did you talk to Rita? Is she okay for tomorrow?" Vinnie moved into the bathroom, which crowded Ben as he changed out of his workout sweats, and hoping to interrupt the ramble about Qasim, Ben's twenty-two-year-old trainee that looked like a missile defense system.

"Three days out and he's shredded. He stands a good chance to place if he works on his posing routine," Ben said as he pushed Vinnie back to disrobe.

Vinnie knew bodybuilding jargon. Three days remained before the competition, and Qasim's extremely low water and body fat caused his shred—exaggerating contour muscle checkered with veins. Qasim had a chest big enough for two and blood vessels to give cardiologists wet dreams. "Good luck to him. Now, about Rita?"

Ben sighed. "We talked." He put his workout clothes in the hamper, then pushed Vinnie out of the bathroom into the bedroom. He slipped into boxer shorts and stretched a skimpy tank top over his head.

"Should I call her? Check in?"

"No, she's good."

"You're sure? What'd you say?" Vinnie rested on the edge of the bed. He could have guessed but wanted to hear Ben say it. He guessed right. The talk was during a workout session, the conversation about weight loads.

"I asked you to talk to Rita, not hurl iron at each other. Ever hear about, oh, I don't know, chatting at a table over a cup of coffee or even a gooey protein shake? Conversation without props."

Ben smiled. "Not Rita's style. And coffee and gooey protein shakes are props." Ben put his arm around Vinnie, mashing his shoulder blades together. "Pumping two hundred pounds is Rita's icebreaker."

"Ball-breaker." Vinnie massaged his shoulder that Ben had pushed. The Chicago trip worried him. "What if she shuts down or goes kung-fuckin'-fu on some guy's ass over a misspoken word?"

Ben's kiss halted Vinnie's growing anxiety, then he pulled Vinnie off the bed with one hand and escorted him to the kitchen. "Let's eat and then go to bed. You have an early start."

***

Supper was okay, bedroom sex great, but sleep impossible. Vinnie rose from the bed while Ben snored. He flipped through Blanca's research report, a generic compilation on teenage suicides. He applied his philosophy.

Kids suffer cruel acts. The resilient survive. Everyone else is earmarked for miserable lives with two choices. One leads to heavy drug and alcohol abuse, broken marriages, or low-paying jobs with the possibility of incarceration until a heart attack, cancer, or dementia ends the misery. The other option truncates the misery, swapping it for the end of a rope, gun barrel, or pharmaceutical bottle.

A perverted homage was offered to the school elite. Coaches, teachers, and school administrators made sacrificial offerings of some so the elite garnered trophies, athletic scholarships, and Ivy League admissions. Talent counted more than middling mediocrity. The pantheon of athletes, brainiacs, and exquisite beauty valued above the clutch of non-athletes, C-students, and plain-lookers. Misfits, sexual nonconformists, cross-dressers, and personalities mismatched with genitalia were invisible or actively reviled.

Vinnie stood, swaying, supporting himself with hands on his chair. He thought about the worst bullying cases. Did the school turn a blind eye when parents produced a large check? Was this the modern equivalent of a plenary indulgence for transgressions? He tried to imagine parental emotions on learning about the abuse heaped with impunity on their child. He failed on emotion but felt their raw anger.

And if he felt angry, then the muggings and murders could conceivably have been committed by a single vengeful parent. Or was Rita right? Could the Ritters or Costermanns or Dellarosas be assassins? Maybe others? What would he do in their situation?

"Blanca, do we know if there are other families with bullied kids?" His recorded message was fast and frenetic.

Message two: "Blanca, we'll need more data for Dan's outliers."

Message three: "Blanca, did you check parents' criminal records?"

Message four: "Blanca, you need to look into adjacent counties, even New York's Rockland County."

Message five: "Blanca, we'll need more data on the socioeconomic status of the bullies and the bullied."

Message six: "Blanca—"

Click, the phone call interrupted. "One more message and I'll bully you into oblivion." Blanca was stern more than angry. "I know what to do and I'll call Dan in the morning, like normal people."

Vinnie went back to bed but still could not sleep. The Costermann interview would be unlike anything he had ever done before.

Chapter 21

Delay and Rita's silence were the two notable events on the American Airlines flight to Chicago. Vinnie was glad he insisted on the early morning departure, which kept him and Rita on time for their appointment with Mr. and Mrs. Costermann.

With seat belt loosened, Vinnie reclined while the plane cruised the thin upper atmosphere. *Ben's right, Rita would not have a conversation across a table. She's hardly said two sentences since we passed through airport security.*

For an hour Vinnie listened to a podcast on professional PI interview techniques with grieving parents. The takeaway points seemed obvious: wait for responses; do not comment or suggest alternative theories; never tell a parent how to act or feel. Agree with everything. *Nothing new. Why do I bother downloading this stuff?*

***

"I will not pretend I'm sorry. I can't. Not after what his daughter did..." John Costermann's lips formed a sneer, his grimace directed at Vinnie, who had described Bob Reinhardt's hunting accident. Vinnie hid the fact that Glen Dingle revealed the details to Rita after sex.

Vinnie and Rita sat in the nondescript Costermann house in a northwest Chicago suburb. A mixed middle- and upper-class community with sufficient minority families to not be all-white, as if the Costermanns had uprooted their entire New Jersey hometown to Illinois. Rita stared at Vinnie, touching his arm. She was nervous, which made him nervous as well.

The house was not a home, but a place where John and Debbie Costermann sheltered. A house Karen would never know—only her photos came to Chicago, remnants of a once happy young girl's life before her premature end. The mantel portrait explained Karen's first "mistake"—to not be born glamorous, magazine-cover beautiful. The portrait dominated the room, which proved Karen was beautiful to John and Debbie. Karen's second "mistake" was to be in the same classroom as Jessica Reinhardt.

John Costermann presented his version of the story, accentuating with intonation the hypocrisy: nothing was his daughter's fault yet a not very subtle suggestion by school administrators was *everything that happened was Karen's doing*. The final straw came when he overheard someone say "suicide was a weak person's way to deal with adversity."

On hearing John's response tinged with sadness and malice, Vinnie said, "I understand."

A scowl formed on John Costermann's face, his eyes widened, the redness spreading over his neck. On his inhale through flared nostrils he held his breath.

"No, I don't mean it like that. I mean my friend was murdered and people suggested he was to blame. I am not comparing my friend's loss to yours. I'm talking about your feelings over Bob Reinhardt. I never felt sorry for my friend's murderer, even when she died. That's what I get."

John relaxed. His face was less of a scowl as he opened his mouth to breathe but said nothing.

Debbie Costermann had sat quietly, listening to her husband, waiting for his weak exhale before she spoke. "We're supposed to be Christians, to forgive, but I can never forgive Bob Reinhardt for not stopping his daughter." Her head shook like a flittering moth.

The story unfolded, beginning with an unfortunate paring of two incompatible personalities. "Karen's sophomore year, she and Jessica were in the same English class," said a now subdued Debbie.

Vinnie and Rita nodded. They listened to Debbie's summary of events as if hearing it for the first time. The bullying by Jessica Reinhardt: the attractive cheerleading captain; the girls' lacrosse and basketball all-star; homecoming queen; ringleader of the vicious Facebook and Twitter campaigns targeting Karen Costermann.

"But didn't you move Karen to a private girls' school?" Rita asked.

"Little good that did." Debbie Costermann teared up, her voice cracking as she continued her daughter's desperate tale. The relentless stalking by Jessica for no apparent reason other than malicious fun, and which made Jessica more powerful and able to control other girls. Debbie speculated on such mean spirit with unbounded denigration. Then she started sobbing once again, her husband holding her hand and trying to soothe her.

"It's still raw no matter how much time passes," said John Costermann, rubbing his wife's shoulder. "We tried to get Bob Reinhardt to stop his daughter."

"We begged. We pleaded for him to take action." Debbie's voice was sour.

"He said he'd talk to her but we knew he was just patronizing us," said John, his bitterness harmonizing with Debbie's. "Reinhardt spent his time picking up women, hunting, and making money by any means possible." He paused. "And word around the school was he had affairs even when his wife was alive."

Rita spoke, her voice low, puffing. "The school?"

"Not much help," answered John.

"But didn't Mrs. McCarthy know? As you said, it started in her English class."

Debbie Costermann walked out of the room and returned cradling a book. "This is Karen's diary. We never looked at it until after... I wish I had."

"Debbie! Stop. We've been over this. No more 'wish we had' and 'if only.'"

Fingering the book, Debbie handed it to Vinnie, a page earmarked. He read and Rita moved closer, her chin resting on his shoulder to read along. Both labored to breathe.

Karen wrote about the single episode that caused her so much misery and eventually led to her suicide. She had farted in English class within Jessica's earshot. That moment was reenacted every time she walked past Jessica: her waving hand, fingers pinching her nose, and calling out, "Rotten eggs in here. Someone open the windows."

Vinnie yelled out, "This is ridiculous, trivial!" He ran a finger over the words.

Debbie took the book from Vinnie and turned the pages. "Read this."

The words in Karen's diary left no doubt that Jessica organized the football team to call their daughter "Karen FF," meaning Farting Fatty.

"It didn't stop when we moved Karen to a private school. Jessica continued to tweet, saying she could 'smell FF across Bergen County.'"

The cruelty hurt. In the diary, Karen had underlined Jessica's hashtag: #FartyK.

Debbie reached for the book and turned to the first-page inscription to read:

Let your imagination take you to faraway places. Create the world you want. I know you will do wonderful things in life.

With best wishes and warmest regards,

Judy McCarthy

"Mrs. Judy McCarthy, the English teacher?" asked Vinnie.

"Yes. Supported Karen. She called a few times and encouraged her to ignore silly girls like Jessica. Terrible what happened to her. A truly lovely person."

The name seemed vaguely familiar to Vinnie. Rita handed him the binder with the spreadsheet. Mrs. Judy McCarthy was listed and like most Lincoln High teachers and staff her cell notes were either unremarkable or blank, except for an X in the columns labeled DECEASED. But no mention of a mugging or a bullying connection. Judy McCarthy had not stayed at Lincoln High. Vinnie ran his fingers across the row with her name. "What happened?" Vinnie's hand covered one eye as Mrs. Costermann explained.

"She left teaching after the football players incident. Do you know about that?"

Vinnie and Rita nodded, and Rita's head bowed to stare at her jogging sneakers.

"We heard she went into software engineering or something like that. Our friends from Mahwah read about her death in the paper, some kind of illness but I can't recall what. They sent us the newspaper clipping. We sent flowers and we would have attended the funeral but we had already moved out here."

"What about the vice principal, Mrs. Wasilewski?" Rita's voice had an edge. She twisted her torso. "Didn't she take steps to stop Jessica?"

"Not really. She told us that student discipline fell to the assistant principal, which was Mrs. McArthur."

John Costermann became suddenly animated, rising from his chair. "Yeah, lot of help McArthur was, goddamn fu—"

Debbie took hold of her husband's forearm before he finished his sentence. "No, stop, John. Don't excite yourself." She turned to Vinnie and Rita. "He's upset, we both are, and this just brings it all back."

"So Mrs. Wasilewski did nothing?" Vinnie said.

Debbie let go of her husband's arm and folded her hands in her lap. "No, although she said she had talked to Jessica and Bob." Vinnie and Rita edged forward as she told them that unidentified complaints had been lodged against Mrs. Wasilewski, complaints that she overstepped her job description as vice principal in pushing Judith McArthur to take action against Jessica.

"Mrs. Wasilewski left Lincoln under duress to become principal at Delmore Girls' Academy," added John.

"Yes, and we were surprised to hear rumors of bullying at Delmore," said Debbie. Both Costermanns had dismissed it as malicious gossip by vindictive parents at Lincoln.

"Mrs. Wasilewski retired and moved to Virginia. Did you know?" Vinnie asked, staring into Debbie Costermann's eyes. Rita checked the spreadsheet notes, her head nodding to confirm Vinnie's facts.

"No, I didn't know that."

"Do you think it possible Mrs. Wasilewski could have done more?" Rita's voice was an uncharacteristic hush, and Vinnie watched her closely. *Was Rita okay?*

Rita took over the questioning, allowing Vinnie to take a break. He returned from the bathroom remarking on the floral bouquet in the hallway table with yellow roses and a single white. He complemented Mrs. Costermann, saying the combination was unusual.

"Yes, they are beautiful. Greg Fine sent them. He always remembers Karen's memorial, the same month his poor wife died of cancer. I met her once."

Before Debbie Costermann had finished, her husband interrupted. "Nice man. He provided Karen's funeral flowers at no charge. You know he owns at least four stores in Bergen County, but the main one is in Mahwah. He's done very well for himself."

"Yes," said Debbie. "Such a gentle, good soul."

The conversation ended with John Costermann checking his watch. "Geez, look at the time. I'm afraid we must wind this up. As I'm sure Debbie told you, we are meeting friends for dinner."

"Yes. So sorry. But call anytime if you have more questions," said Debbie, almost cheerful.

***

From his hotel room, Vinnie updated Blanca and asked for more data. On the LaGuardia flight he switched seats with Rita. Staring out the window at passing clouds reminded him of invisible forces. His mind gritted over a different invisible force, sinister and, like the flight, nonstop.

Make It Count

Chapter 22

A short column in the *Washington Post*, page eight, section II, detailed the murder at Newport News near the US Naval Base, a location considered a safe haven to enjoy some of Virginia's magnificent beaches. The *Bergen Record* did not cover the incident but posted an obituary. Blanca discovered the *Post* article after Vinnie's phone request for more information. She took a day to find it, but tapped the newspaper printout to get Vinnie's attention. A yellow marker highlighted the murder victim's name.

"This can't be right!" Vinnie took the paper, bringing it closer to his face. Despite the winter snow, he came to work without a coat, riding the elevator from his condo to the BIG office. Blanca, who arrived on the Long Island Railroad, stored her LL Bean boots under her desk and flung her down ski jacket onto the office coat rack.

She walked barefoot to Vinnie, grabbing the page. "It's in the paper so it must be true, right?" Her smile contrasted with her frantic page-waving.

"It's not right. Everyone said she was nice."

Vinnie looked at the snowy gray sky, a New York January. Why did he leave sunny San Francisco? His sore inner thighs reminded him of the previous night with Ben, and he remembered.

"So? Nice or nasty is not the point." Blanca barked her response. She had made an interview appointment at Delmore Girls' Academy for the following day to get the official version on Mrs. Wasilewski.

"Bullshit."

"What's bullshit?" said Rita entering the office and hearing Vinnie. In her tai chi outfit she looked ready for a street fight. Her face had a polished porcelain sheen.

Blanca showed Rita the printout, then pushed Vinnie away from the computer to pull up the *Bergen Record* web page. A short article reported Delmore Girls' Academy principal and former Lincoln High vice principal Mrs. Michelina Wasilewski's retirement, an educator of some thirty years.

An older article referenced an unnamed student's overdose at Delmore Academy. The story focused on the teenager's drug use from the human-interest angle, and mentioned none of Debbie Costermann's gossip about bullying.

Rita looked at Vinnie. "Remember that's the Delmore rumor Mrs. Costermann called 'malicious gossip,' right?"

Muttering disbelief, Vinnie's words were a squall like a winter snowstorm. "Forget the Delmore interview. Schools will have a snow day tomorrow by the looks of it."

"So now what?" Rita paced, twisted, and cracked her neck bones. Vinnie shuddered on hearing the popping cartilage. It seemed that Rita was back.

"A lot of work, that's what. We screwed up." Vinnie scratched at his cheek.

They divided the assignments up. Blanca would look into disciplinary complaints at Delmore Academy. Vinnie and Rita would partition interviews among Michelina Wasilewski's family. As a widow of many years with no children, all she had were a few blood relatives and former in-laws. To tieup loose ends someone would talk to the former English teacher Judy McCarthy's widower.

"The Jim McCarthy interview is in a few days. Hopefully we won't have a blizzard." Based on Vinnie's Chicago phone call, Blanca made this her first priority, even before the now cancelled Delmore appointment. Mr. McCarthy was away on business, and his return flight was scheduled at the end of the week.

Palms pressed as if in prayer, Vinnie aimed two index fingers pushed together at Rita. "You want to do it?"

With a smoked gaze Rita pointed to herself. "Me? Alone with a widower? Can I be trusted?"

Vinnie and Blanca had a long discussion over this decision, reaching the conclusion that words of confidence in Rita without action were empty.

"To his home for an interview in chairs, not a bed." A wisp of a smile flashed over Vinnie's face.

Blanca scowled. "So much for subtle, *pendejo.*"

***

Not a single disparaging word was said against Michelina Wasilewski. Vinnie and Blanca reported that no one had heard of bullying at Delmore Academy. The in-laws loved her and had kept in close contact after the fatal car accident that took her husband, their brother, at the age of thirty-five. She never remarried, and the overall consensus concluded that that was a pity. Michelina's siblings described her as the best sister anyone could ever have, adored by the nieces and nephews.

They hoped Rita might gain more insight from Jim McCarthy.

"Now isn't this ironic?" Vinnie looked at Blanca with Rita sitting behind him.

The women looked at each other, shrugging their shoulders.

"You know, we're disturbed this victim was considered a good person?"

Blanca started to speak, but stopped. Rita gave a slight nod, saying, "Yes, we expected all victims in this case had done something bad or were themselves bad people."

Vinnie looked to both women. "Does this make Mrs. Wasilewski an outlier?"

"And are we becoming cynical like Debbie and John Costermann?" Rita's voice was confessional as she left the office followed by Vinnie.

An hour later Vinnie called Blanca. His voice stumbled with the rapidity of his words. Using Google Earth he had located a convenience store in Newport News across from the scene of Michelina's murder. Blanca didn't understand his excitement until he continued.

"The store has an external camera." He knew chances were slim that the camera functioned, let alone that someone had kept old recordings. "Apply your charm and find out." Vinnie slowed to pronounce *El Almacén*, a specialty bodega.

"Vinnie, *Estás lleno de mierda*—full of shit. My charm being Puerto Rican?"

"And you such a charming Puerto Rican, especially when you talk dirty."

Blanca waited to tell Vinnie in person. Not only did the cameras function, but the Newport News detectives had looked at the footage. They came up empty on the Wasilewski murder. The bodega owner reused the memory space but turned out to be paranoid, so for legal protection made a backup. He promised to include a copy with Blanca's order of three imported Arroz con Gandules cans.

"It will cost you about seventy-five bucks and change including postage," she said smiling and rapid eyelid blinking.

"And why do we need pigeon peas and chorizo?"

"To make the owner more agreeable. And Al loves it. With the hours you make me work I don't have the time to make that shit from scratch."

"Lazy, aren't we?"

Blanca's middle finger stuck up so high it nearly touched the ceiling.

The video footage played. Vinnie pointed to the screen, turned to Blanca, asking about the white van in the lot across from the bodega. The van arrived forty-five minutes before Michelina's murder. Vinnie's Google Map estimate placed the parking lot three hundred feet from the bodega front door.

"What do you think?" Vinnie sat back. "Similar to the van we saw at Lincoln High?"

Blanca moved closer to the screen. "Could be, but there's no insignia, at least not visible from this angle. The vehicle tags look like Jersey plates but it's impossible to read." Lots of states' vanity plates looked the same, using landmarks, colors, and vanity words to earn state income.

"Can you read the plate?" Vinnie pushed away, making space for Blanca.

"*Nada.*"

"Darken the image."

Blanca adjusted the contrast. A few letters became visible.

"Not much. Looks like L, U, something something or blank, something something S?"

"Damn. LUV BEES. Is that it?"

"Could be. Why?"

Vinnie reclined, startled by Blanca's outburst. "Look!" She tapped the screen. "Isn't that the same guy who walked into the shop twenty minutes prior to the murder and now entering the van?"

Vinnie squinted. He paused the video to enlarge the image, distorting the pixels. He reduced the size five points and a black baseball-style cap took shape, but the brim insignia was illegible. "That looks familiar. A flower? Tulip?"

"Could be. I can't tell." Blanca adjusted the screen size several times, both larger and smaller. "Look, underneath the tulips. See it? Looks like double Fs."

Vinnie screamed out, "O-M-G. Order a bouquet from Fine Flowers." Vinnie's voice was upbeat. He was hugging Blanca and she pushed him away.

"What the fuck, Vinnie? Why so excited?"

"Don't you get it? The license plate, the insignia on the cap, the white van. I've seen all of these like five or six times all over NJ, and they are the flowers delivered in every house we've interviewed, even the Costermanns in Chicago."

They knew not to have the flowers delivered to the office and so considered UltraFit, but decided Fine Flowers would FTD them from a local Manhattan florist anyway. Vinnie remembered a Marriott in Mahwah, and Blanca reserved a room so she could have the flowers delivered to the front desk. Her thought was for a crystal vase at one-twenty-five that would look great on her dining room table. Vinnie mumbled a curse, revising the value to "Fifty bucks in a box." He paused. "And make it for a dozen yellow roses with a single white."

Blanca didn't get it, but before she could ask for an explanation, Rita walked in asking questions. She was ready for her Saturday interview with Jim McCarthy but wanted to go over one or two points. Vinnie told her of the change in plan and held up his hand to stop her from complaining. The new plan was for her to check in to the Mahwah Marriott and retrieve a box of flowers. If that threw her off-guard, she glazed over when told to check in as Blanca Santos. The kicker was she would not stay overnight, but proceed to the McCarthy interview. Rita remained silent, both hands on her face for a few seconds. As she started to repeat the instructions, Vinnie interrupted to say he forgot to mention he would be outside the Marriott watching her from the parking lot.

Rita raised her hands in the air, lifting her shoulders. "Whatever you say, boss. I have no clue." She looked up to see Vinnie's grin.

"What!" she demanded.

Vinnie's parting directive required Rita to call the Costermanns for a simple confirmation. He closed the door. "I've got to prepare my equipment."

"Really, again with you and Ben?" Blanca shook her head.

"Camera equipment. My other's always prepared."

Vinnie frowned leaving the room, hiding his smile until the door closed, and he lingered for a moment to bask in the women's laughter.

***

"I spoke to Mrs. Costermann," said Rita with eyebrows rising.

Vinnie's constant interruptions delayed Rita's summary. Mrs. Debbie Costermann talked with hubby John, deciding in retrospect that Mrs. Wasilewski may have been duplicitous and selective in the bullies she disciplined. They had ignored grapevine gossip at the time, which suggested Michelina Wasilewski negotiated the settlement for the football players' families, the kids that beat up a freshman.

"Debbie didn't recall their names until I suggested Jeff Dellarosa." Rita thought she heard shock in Mrs. Costermann's voice at the revelation.

"Here's the new bit. Emily Dingle, wife of my former lover Glen," Rita coughed, "was the vice principal for student discipline but resigned her post when her son started at Lincoln High, making way for Wasilewski. Turns out the women were close friends."

Vinnie blurted out, "We've been handed horse shit all along! Even your former lover wasn't open with you after all your fucking." He relaxed his jaw, dropped his head, and closed his eyes. "I'm sorry, Rita. I shouldn't have said that." He waited until she nodded, and Vinnie's voice lowered. "I'm afraid one woman died from a mistake and another will follow. It's not for us to judge whether she deserved it. We have to stop the madness but we need more evidence. Let's hope the answer comes from flowers and Jim McCarthy."

Chapter 23

"This is very interesting."

"Maybe to you. I don't see a fu... a fudgin' thing." Vinnie sat next to Dan, both men staring at the computer screen.

"Look. Each location within the school zone and each victim is connected to Lincoln High, even if not at the time of their murder. All similar except one."

"You mean Bob Reinhardt?"

"Exactly."

"Because his daughter had graduated from Lincoln High by the time we have the first murder?"

"No, because Bob Reinhardt is the only male victim. And death by bullet, not by metal club."

"Hmm."

"Yes, but the dead wife and daughter change everything. He's less of an anomaly and more of an outlier."

Vinnie groaned.

***

The twenty-story condominium complex smelled of money starting with the lobby's walnut concierge's desk. Pushing the elevator button, Rita read the notices locked behind glass: Sign up with Nestor for the Memorial Day barbecue; Semi-annual pool cleaning closure; Reminder to reserve tennis courts with Ramon a day in advance; Welcome our two new personal trainers and schedule a free one-hour session.

Inside the walnut-paneled elevator, Rita had just learned the inhabitants were fit and wealthy. She knocked on the condo door, turning to examine the recently carpeted hallway and the modern art prints mounted on freshly painted walls.

An expressionless, handsome man peered out of the half-open door. A smile would have made him unbearably beautiful.

"Hello, Mr. McCarthy, I'm Rita Light from Briggs Investigative Group. I believe you spoke to the BIG assistant Blanca Santos. Is this still a good time?"

The door swung open and he said, "Of course. Please, come in." A six-foot man stood before her. Rita liked him even before crossing the threshold. She didn't stare, she grazed, sizing him up in brief, casual glances: short-sleeve shirt outlining impressive pectorals, bicep-bunched sleeves, buck-wide shoulders pulling seams. Mineral blue eyes above a short delicate nose that perfectly fitted the deliciously symmetrical face. Rita restrained herself from entangling her fingers in the tawny, lion-mane hair, pulling his head back, and kissing that perfect mouth.

She knew two things before the door closed. Jim McCarthy used the condo gym a lot, and if he wasn't careful she would gift wrap the twenty-eight-year-old and cart him home as a room ornament.

"May I offer you something to drink? Tea, coffee, water?"

"Thanks, Mr. McCarthy, water's good." *And a fuck.*

"Jim, please."

"Okay. I'm Rita." *And I fuck real good.*

The interview began with Jim answering low-ball questions about his job and general health. With a begrudged grin, he replied that he either was at work or worked out in the gym. Rita couldn't confirm the former but believed the latter. He sipped his water on every mention of his wife's name. He lamented his error for not being home for a final goodbye before she went off for a school party, never to return. He finished his water and went for a refill.

Rita sat up. "Wait. Why would that matter? I mean... well, didn't she die of an illness?"

Jim McCarthy appeared to smile until his upper teeth clenched on his lower lip. With a sharp "No," he stopped. Then apologized for his rudeness. The obituary listing was illness, but his wife had been beaten into a coma, and died after just short of a month in hospital.

Rita's face whitened as capillaries constricted around her cheeks, mouth, and neck.

The more the topic dwelled on his wife the more Jim's adoration swelled. He married Judy out of desire, friendship, and love. He was now wedded to a job to forget and to exercise to fend off loneliness. He sold their Mahwah home, collected Judy's life insurance, and purchased the one-bedroom high-end condo. Enough remained to invest and allow him to quit his job to live off dividends.

"Then what? Become more depressed? Alcohol or drugs? Judy would not have..." He teared up. "I have a fantastic New York skyline view and sit alone. I don't go out. Why would I without Judy? At least I'm away from that suburban house and... the memories." His voice sunk and he drank his water.

The McCarthys' matchup was too clichéd to not be true. They met at university, he in computer science and she in education with an English specialty. As a work-study student, Jim received Judy's frantic call that she had deleted the entire English department's files. Jim's chuckle broke his disconsolate discourse allowing a grin to rake his face as he described his rush through the door and Judy's rush out. They collided, knocking skulls, and themselves into semi-consciousness on the ground.

"We told people we were star-struck, literally. We married a year later."

His tears flowed, shoulders slumped. Jim McCarthy sank into a new leather chair opposite the matching sofa where Rita sat. He muttered. Human behavior confounded him. That someone would bash Judy's head in with a metal pole made no sense. "She wasn't robbed or raped, just put into a coma and dead in a month." He cried and covered his face.

Gaining control, he pointed to a class photograph. "Everyone liked Judy. She had been at Lincoln High a short time but earned best teacher award from her students and—" The crying took hold of him and he left the room.

On reentering, he apologized. "No need," said Rita. She saw his stare. Was he looking at her in that way? She sat upright, brushing her short red hair, her gesture drawing attention to the light tan of her arms and neck. Although she did not wear lipstick, water droplets moistened her lips, which parted to expose white leopard-long incisors.

"More?" he asked, pointing to Rita's empty glass.

"No, thanks. Sit next to me."

He returned to his chair, leaning away from Rita.

After a lull, Jim continued to talk about Judy. Rita interrupted. The interview agenda had changed. This was new information relevant to the investigation. She asked different questions to those she had prepared.

She learned Judy McCarthy changed career, unable to coexist with her conscience and school politics. She could not abide that vulnerable students sank into abject misery caused by their bullying peers. She became disgusted with school administrators swayed by parents with power and money. She abandoned teaching. Jim chuckled. "Ironically, she joined a computer firm and wrote manuals." He laughed for the first time. "She edited engineers' reports and said she wished she had them in her English class." His lilt vanished and he stopped talking.

Rita waited, but knew further discussion of Judy McCarthy was closed. Sadness silkscreened Jim's face. Rita ached. Love had graced this man until fickle cruelty took it away. She waited. "Tell me Jim, have you dated? Are you seeing anyone?"

"What? No, I... no."

"You're a good-looking man. Why not?"

"Why not?" repeated Jim. He looked confused.

Rita stopped. Jim yielded to the long silence, admitting a few women had made friendly gestures. Young and old, attractive and not so much, single and married, and the pool lifeguard. Rita thought, if he told her he had fifty offers she'd think it an underestimate. An older, married colleague told him any woman in the office was his for the asking. She advised Jim to date, get out there. It would do him good.

"How does anyone know what would do me good? A friend said the same to me and I was mad at him for two weeks." He paused. "I knew he only meant well, but meaning well and helping are not the same."

"You've decided to remain single? Is that it?"

Rita knew her question was too direct, unrelated to the investigation. A personal-interest question. She expected a sharp response but received a weak smile, watching his head moving side to side. She apologized and Jim waved her off, saying he felt he could talk freely with her. Maybe because she was a stranger. He didn't know why.

Nodding in agreement with his vague conclusion, Rita peered into Jim's half-closed eyes. She knew. Her nod was not for understanding but from passion. She wanted to have sex with him. Her thighs twitched, a heat filled her chest, and her throat tightened.

Jim's eyes and neck tilted up to the ceiling. "Judy was my first." He paused, a smile pulled his lips apart. "I was a virgin when I met Judy. Imagine at twenty-two and I was still a virgin? I'm sure she wasn't, but I never asked."

A big smile crossed Rita's face, her teeth elongated ready to lunge and take hold of his lips.

"It's funny, isn't it? I was a sheltered child and adolescent. I had feelings for girls in high school but I was too shy to act on them. I didn't attend my prom. At college I heard the dormitory banter and locker room gossip. I had no experience. An unsophisticated geek. I didn't even know how to ask for a date. Bumping a girl's head was my pickup line."

Rita burst into a loud staccato laugh and he joined her.

"I'm sorry, Jim, I meant no offense."

"No offense taken. It feels good to laugh."

"Jim, honestly, say hello and you'll have any woman if she's breathing. You are a very attractive man."

Without asking, he described his marriage, as if talking brought Judy back to life. Jim revealed that his wife had orchestrated their first sexual encounter, and with a self-deprecating chuckle said Judy grasped that he had no clue about what he was doing. "I mean, I understood how the parts fit together but... uh." He burst out laughing with Rita joining him.

"And you have no desire now?" Rita realized she was getting too psychological, too much about Jim. She was off script.

"I feel that sex would betray Judy, be unfair to her. Yes, I have desires... but who would want me? I cry at the slightest thought of her. I'm not even sure how to make love anymore."

Rita made a hasty exit, pretending she had lost track of time and was late for an appointment. She was within seconds of disrobing and draping her naked body over every inch of Jim McCarthy. She thought her heat would ignite the wood-paneled elevator as she descended to the lobby.

Rita returned to the UltraFit parking garage, retrieving the floral box from the passenger seat floor. She entered UltraFit commando style, with a rapid change to workout gear, followed by a brief warm-up. Jim McCarthy's last words were imprinted on her brain. The X-room door burst open as she entered and reconnoitered the bodies on display.

Chapter 24

Prime beef everywhere Rita looked, hernias just a grunt away. Knees popped near to shattering. Testicles moved upward as if the men consumed their own illicit sweetbreads.

She stalked the room. *The hunt is on.* The McCarthy interview had unnerved her. Why did Jim turn out to be gorgeous and needed just what she could offer? Mind-blowing sex. She could satisfy both their needs.

She settled on two prospects. Neither beautiful like Jim but not ugly. The younger one was in his early twenties, the older nearer thirty. Both had buns twice risen, Clydesdale thighs, and alpha biceps. Rita stood over the bench, glaring at the younger man pressing hard while the older spotted. She selected the young one, shorter than her by at least five inches and not as massive as his training partner. But his potential evident. In a few years the youngster would be more muscular and earn a pro-bodybuilding card before hitting thirty. She liked his style. Didn't Jim say he had been a virgin at twenty-two? This guy was no virgin, but he still had much to learn—and she had much to teach the young buck.

Without objection, Rita wormed into the men's routine. On the bench press she pushed a barbell fifty pounds lighter than the young man's poundage, sure this would not dent his masculinity. A few years before she would have pressed a hundred pounds heavier. Her full extension pushed her tits out, along with both men's eyeballs.

After thirty minutes the young stud accepted Rita's invitation for a private tour of her UltraFit office. Neither hesitated over Ben's non-soliciting rule or worried about his fury if he found out. They were juiced. Workout sweat pooled into the man's muscular eight-pack and ran down his arms. A film glistened on Rita's neck and over her breasts to moisten her hard nipples. She threw her bra and panties onto the man's jockstrap and shorts, already discarded on the floor. If necessary they would peel their skin off.

The undressing was the entirety of their foreplay. The young buck was flat on his back in the space behind her desk, the chair flung into a corner of the room. Rita jumped on him like a diving cormorant, yelling out, "OFF!"

"Huh? But you're on me?"

"Open the Fan Fuck. OFF."

"What?"

"Quiet. Just follow."

And he did.

Using her height advantage, Rita threw a leg up going over the young man's shoulder, put her hand under his chin to steady herself as her heel rested next to his ears. The young man became a spectator, except for his large throbbing penis. He jolted as Rita's free hand extended beneath his crouch to mine his anus with two fingers. She shoved a breast into his mouth to stifle his scream. "For fuck's sake, be quiet."

"Mrrph."

"Stand up. Let's do Lord of Dancers Fuck."

The young bodybuilder followed instructions, his clueless expression making Rita smile. For a man who spent the better part of his adult life examining his body in front of wall-to-ceiling mirrors, he seemed unclear what was his and what was hers. He stared at Rita's waxed pussy, polished like a Ferrari.

"Go ahead, touch it."

The bodybuilder's artificial eggplant tan contrasted with Rita's smooth light brown. Her eyes closed, better to imagine the gorgeous Jim McCarthy as a college freshman. Her internal furnace cranked, self-immolation imminent. She moved the young man's hand to her breast and knelt between his legs, examining his launch-ready erection. With a handlebar reach, she opened her desk's supply drawer. *Who keeps sex lubricant and a condom in their desk? What's wrong with me?*

She lubed the young man's shaft, then rimmed his ass, priming for a twenty-thousand-miles open-road thrust. The bodybuilder suckling Rita's nipples stifled his cries as she splayed her fingers inside, cleaning his anus, her long fingers driving past his prostate on the way to heaven. He passed the test drive.

Rita turned around, pulled him inside her, his strong arms wrapped around her, but she controlled the speed. She held him from climax until they both screamed together.

Spent from the sex and two hours' weight lifting, the bodybuilder collapsed. He puppy whimpered, "Oh fuck... so fucking great... I never..."

Rita smiled. She'd fucked him like he'd never been fucked before, making him a virtual virgin, turning him into the twenty-two-year-old Jim McCarthy.

As the youngster picked up his clothes, Rita pulled him to her. She didn't take slam, bam, thank you mam from anyone; like her yoga class, she decided when a session was over. She secured her hands to his man tits, ass sliding along his legs, testicles pushed aside. The bodybuilder jolted.

"Rim my pussy, like you're searching for small diamonds in a box."

He gently explored, slow, his pro-card ready to print. On further instruction, he hoisted himself, as if doing pushups. She kicked his legs apart, ass spread, the AC breeze cooling his rectum. Once more he was inside her, moaning, penis excavating. Rita grabbed his balls, pulling them like a slingshot, hearing his pain, excruciating, joyous. Her palm jelly-rolled his testicles, her labia skated his groin. Her firm tits flattened against his mountainous chest. His arms quivered, a release inevitable. Rita grabbed his pectorals like subway straps, held him airborne, the truth revealed: she could bench press more than him.

With his head nuzzled into her, he went deeper. He sobbed as he ejaculated a second time, spewing cum, his testicles emptying. He rocked with each release. Rita's eyes brightened, her smile elongated, her desire satiated. The feel-good lasted as long as it took to dress. The bowlegged bodybuilder retreated, somewhat shell-shocked.

In the empty office, regret returned. She could have satisfied Jim had she not acted irresponsibly with Glen. It would have worked with Jim. No children. No secret to guard.

As a PI she had only uncovered her loneliness and pathological sex addiction. No amount of tae kwon do, yoga, or gym time could change the facts: she lured men into sex. *Why*? Then the inevitable question, *What is wrong with me*?

The specter of Jim McCarthy would not leave. He persisted, nagged, an unrelenting silhouette in her mind's eye. He loved Judy, desperate to be true to her memory. In contrast, Rita wanted to erase all memory of her former bastard ex. Jim knew Judy loved him. Did her ex-partner ever love her? Judy was popular with students and respected by colleagues. *Who respects me? Am I popular? Does anyone actually like me?* Rita glanced at the closed office door that minutes before had framed a youth, the sawtooth blade of serrated muscles, and the truth was clear. He wanted sex, and liking her didn't matter.

She sat. Stood. Paced. Sat again. Jim McCarthy's sorrow had permeated his body. He had loved and lost. He deserved to know the why and who. She couldn't help him. She could not sublimate her sexual desire.

This case fueled her perverse emotions, even if laced with empathy. Rita was torn. She liked Jim and wanted sex with him, but even if she applied all her willpower she didn't think herself capable or strong enough to stop herself. Her palms rubbed at her forehead, as if smoothing out the creases there would help. She put the sex lubricant away and discarded the condoms.

She looked around, then at her computer she typed a summary of her interview, detailing all she had learned about Judy McCarthy. She would then compose a second resignation letter, which would be irrevocable.

1. Fact: JM was murdered, and had not died from an illness.

2. Fact: JM did not fit the revenge theory, making her murder capricious.

3. Fact: JM did not support bullies regardless of social or economic status.

4. Fact: JM was well liked.

5. Fact: JM told her about Jessica Reinhardt's bullying case, besides the Karen Costermann incident. (Who?)

6. Impression: At Lincoln High everyone knew something and no one knew everything. What?

7. Impression: Bob Reinhardt's murder was different, a long-distance shot not the close-up blow with a metal rod. His exploding head eradicated his identity.

8. Speculation: One victim per family or was this cycling among members? A spouse, then the other, then a child? Other, then children? Jessica, Brett, and Ken next?

9. Speculation: If this is about bullying, why not punish the bully? Why specific teachers and principals and not others?

She'd deliver her list and resignation letter in the morning. A quick aerosol spray dispersed the lingering sex odor and she closed up the office for the night. At home, Rita's body crawled into bed but not her mind. She turned on the bed lamp, reached for her list and wrote in pen.

Why was vice principal Judith McArthur spared?

Nearly midnight in New York, an hour earlier in Chicago. Rita picked up her cell phone and made a call. A bright voice answered.

"Hello, Mrs. Costermann, this is Rita Light. I hope this is not too late?"

"No, dear, not at all. I don't go to bed until one or two. I watch a few shows and read. I don't sleep much."

"This will only take a few minutes. I want to follow up on Mrs. McCarthy and also Mrs. McArthur."

In the few minutes Rita confirmed what she learned from Jim McCarthy. Judy McCarthy was well liked, while Judith McArthur had mixed reviews because the general opinion was she favored the popular kids, the star athletes, the top academics, and the wealthy. She didn't show much interest in students that were mediocre, not involved in high school activities, or unattractive.

"And what about the Fine family? Did you ever keep up with them?"

"As I told you and Vinnie, our girls weren't close. What a tragedy, too, about Dawn. That poor man. He's lost so much."

"You mean his wife?"

"Yes. But also Dawn, his daughter."

Rita waited.

"Her overdose."

"What?"

"The Fines' only child, Dawn, died of an overdose."

"What? I don't remember you mentioning this. Where? And when?"

"A few years back at Delmore Girls' Academy. She transferred the year before Mrs. Wasilewski became principal."

Did Jim mention any of this? Rita did not sleep until nearly two but planned to arrive at BIG before Vinnie or Blanca, right after her kick-ass UltraFit tae kwon do class.

Chapter 25

Vinnie glared from his swivel chair to Rita seated on the other side of his desk. "Come on, Rita, again with the 'I quit' bullshit?" He looked around the room. "Look at how much you've uncovered and deduced." He swung her notes in the air, tossing her resignation letter into a corner wastebasket. Vinnie cupped his hands, saying words he never imagined he could utter. "We need you."

Rita burst out laughing, her voice loud. The office door was flung open, Blanca running into the room. "*¡Madre mía!*" She looked to Rita first then Vinnie. "What's going on?"

"Relax," said Vinnie, face flushed. "I made a joke."

Blanca's forehead creased and her eyes narrowed. "Like I can fly."

"It's okay. Vinnie complimented me," Rita said with the remnants of a smile. She repeated Vinnie's comment.

Blanca sat down, smiling at Vinnie. "I take back everything bad I've ever said about you."

"Gosh, Bambina, so sweet of you." Vinnie raised his middle finger.

Blanca turned to Rita. "He's right and that's rare." Not turning, her arm swung to her side, middle finger pointed at Vinnie. "Your investigative work has improved. Still a few bumps—"

Rita snorted. "Bumps? I've had fewer bumps with a guy hanging upside down in a swing."

Vinnie laughed then covered his mouth on Blanca's stare. Rita acknowledged her sex proclivity. "It's hard to explain. Something triggers, like a craving or... I don't know, and then I prowl for a man. But more than sex, I need to take control. Can you get that?"

Vinnie leaned forward. "Yeah, and my guess is it's probably..."

"Vin... in... in... ie!" Blanca's tremolo took two seconds to finish.

"No, go on, say it," said Rita.

Vinnie looked to Blanca and shrugged. "Probably hormonal—is that politically incorrect?"

With hands on hips, Blanca shouted, "What's wrong with you?!"

"No," interrupted Rita, "he's right, not the hormonal bit but the reason. I need help. Depression's one part, although, if I'm honest, my sex drive has always been up there." She lifted an arm straight above her head as a visual aid.

"Wait, I'll get you a stepladder," Vinnie offered with a droll snicker.

Rita burst into an energetic laugh. "Maybe it's my diet."

"You think? Can I have your grocery list for Ben?"

The women's laughter was loud and buoyant. Blanca suggested they give it a rest and take a break. Vinnie stood, crossing his legs. "About fuckin' time. I'm going to pee my pants with all the coffee I've drunk." He heard their howling as he rushed out the door.

Vinnie returned to perch on the edge of his desk peering down on Rita and Blanca seated in front. "Enough on Rita's... err, well... later." He waved his hand at her. "Let's review your points and agree your resignation officially nullified," and pointed to the wastebasket.

Rita's expanded summary had Vinnie rocking in his chair, while Blanca held her forehead looking at her feet.

***

The car parked outside the flower shop. Vinnie reviewed his thoughts but Rita continued to debate the idea of him doing the interview solo. She repeated her main concern. "The man's six foot two, barrel-chested, and surrounded by cutting shears, twine, and metal poles."

Vinnie agreed she was hired to protect him but protested. "I doubt he'll attack me at his place of business with witnesses around." He looked at his side mirror with his hand on the car door handle. "Besides, my reason beats yours."

"And what's that?"

"Greg Fine might reveal things to me alone that he would not say with you present. No witness to corroborate."

"What if he thinks you're wearing a wire?"

"Infrared detectors... kidding. He'll frisk me or ask me or say he objects to being recorded."

"And just saying it works?"

"No, but people think it does."

Vinnie entered the shop, noticing the Fine Flowers employees by their aprons. Three assistants were advising customers. A young man shuffled by with a large planter box. An elderly male at a side desk wrapped a floral bouquet as the customer scribed a note.

"Can I help you?" asked a woman in her early twenties, big smile, pleasant voice. Vinnie imagined she was checking him out. *Yes, I'd be a good catch for you if I wasn't gay.* "I'd like to speak to Greg." Vinnie used the first name to imply friendship with the proprietor or at least that he was a regular client of the florist.

"Oh, sure. I'll see if he's available. Who should I say is calling?"

"Say a mutual friend of Judith McArthur."

During the wait, Vinnie strolled past a series of five-foot-high glass pedestals topped with floral baskets and distributed like sentries throughout the forty by seventy-foot showroom. Price tags ranged from forty dollars for a boutonniere to fifteen hundred for an "arboretum" in a hand-painted ceramic vase half the height of an adult man.

"Ah, Mr. Briggs. Please come to my office. I've been expecting you. We were not formally introduced by Doris in the Lincoln High faculty parking lot."

Vinnie thought, *I'm in a movie. This way, Mr. Bond. Pussy Galore will now serve you a poisonous cocktail.* "Sure."

They walked behind the desk into a long room lined with large metal tables. "We do the big jobs here. Funerals, weddings, special occasions."

"Good to know." Vinnie felt like a new employee. On one side was a door leading to a small room. Greg Fine pointed to a tall, square metal work table with four high wooden stools on each side. He closed the door as Vinnie sat on the nearest.

"Before we begin, let's dispense with an unpleasantness. Mr. Briggs, are you wearing a wire or a recording device? If so, I do not approve of being recorded and I want to make that clear."

Bingo. "Nope. Clothes and flesh. Care to look?" Vinnie moved to unbutton his shirt and Greg Fine motioned him to stop. "No? I've been working out. Worth the view. And call me Vinnie since we're being intimate. That okay, Greg?"

A barking laugh resounded in the room. "I've heard about your humor, Vinnie. Now, let's see how I can help you."

There was no admission forthcoming. Vinnie heard about Greg Fine's only child, his precious Dawn tormented by bullying, slandered and vilified on Facebook, Twitter, and in other ways. Dawn had been shunned by nearly everyone at Lincoln High, even her two former best friends. Her transfer to Delmore Academy did not abate the online bullying. "But you know all this," Greg concluded.

Vinnie nodded.

"Good," Greg Fine continued. "Now imagine a beautiful young woman." Greg paused, then continued. "Smooth, silky white skin, flowing golden blonde hair, long sinewy legs, ample bosom, tight ass, and a delicate upturned nose. Add athletic and A-student. Got it?"

Vinnie nodded.

"Then you are imagining Jessica Reinhardt."

In contrast, Greg described his daughter Dawn: overweight, round-faced, stringy brown hair, a mediocre C-student, and non-athletic. But a heart of pure gold. He and his wife loved her more than he could describe. Greg Fine sighed, wiping at his eyes. "You know about her overdose?"

Vinnie nodded, his throat dry.

The story shifted to Mrs. Fine's cancer-riddled body. Her last months of pure hell, too weak to support Dawn. Prior to her illness, Dawn's schooling was monitored by Mrs. Fine, and Mr. Fine never felt a need to attend parent–teacher conferences. His expanding florist business was all-consuming with eighty-hour work weeks. When his wife became near incapacitated, she finally told him that it was bullying that caused Dawn's sulky demeanor, which he had assumed was down to typical teenage moodiness. Fury raged, and Greg Fine tried to meet the vice principal for student discipline, but poor timing changed everything. A major bank business loan and the vice principal away for a week-long conference that backed on to the spring break delayed their meeting until after the holiday.

Mrs. Fine died during the spring break. Weeks after the funeral, Greg Fine called Bob Reinhardt, leaving messages with his secretary. After a week Reinhardt returned the call. He scoffed and suggested he put his daughter on a diet and enroll her at a gym.

"No sympathy for my loss, even though his wife died exactly like mine. The self-centered son-of-a-bitch. No wonder his daughter's so rotten."

Vinnie's bile stuck in his gullet. He detested the dead Bob Reinhardt.

"Principal Wasilewski promised she'd look into the matter." Greg Fine sighed. "Patronizing liar. The school year finished and I transferred Dawn to Delmore Academy." He sighed. "Didn't matter. Jessica pursued Dawn on social media. A year later Mrs. Wasilewski was Delmore's new principal. Another kick in the teeth for Dawn."

"And the overdose was that same year?"

"Overdose!" Greg's face turned red, his voice at near scream level. "The fucking overdose was suicide. I didn't tell the police but Dawn left a note. No one but me has seen it."

"I'm so sorry. That is truly terrible."

"If only Mrs. McCarthy had taken my call, applied pressure to stop Jessica."

"You mean Mrs. McArthur?"

"What? No, Judy McCarthy, the vice principal for student discipline."

"But Judy McCarthy was an English teacher."

"*The Record* quoted Mrs. McCarthy as the vice principal for student discipline in their high school bullying exposé series. They quoted her statement on Lincoln High's zero-tolerance policy. Mrs. McCarthy lied to the newspaper."

"That was a misprint. *The Record* posted a correction but not until a week later." Vinnie knew because Blanca's research discovered the correction, and corrections are buried on back pages.

"What? No. You're wrong." Greg Fine pitched sideways, his face bloated. He stretched for the table to stop his stool from overturning.

"You never met Mrs. McArthur? You never knew her name?"

"I don't remember. It was before my wife died. I just asked to speak with the disciplinary vice principal... I was angry. Maybe I didn't pay close attention." His eyes turned inward, his hand covered his mouth. "No... oh, God." He stood, walked to the front of the cutting table, and slammed his fist into the metal top. "Who did you say Mrs. McCarthy was?"

"An English teacher. She left Lincoln over disagreement with their policy. She went to work at a computer firm. Students voted her best teacher. Five hundred people attended her funeral Mass."

Greg Fine kicked his stool and sent it crashing across the room. "Leave, NOW!"

Vinnie hesitated, and the man moved to the rear of the table to select another stool to throw across the room into a wall. A young employee ran into the room. "Mr. Fine, is everything okay?" The young man looked at Vinnie skeptically.

"Out! Everyone get the fuck out now! Leave!" Greg Fine's back bent over to form a half-shell, his hand covered his face. Vinnie thought he heard the man mumbling but it could have been sobbing.

***

Vinnie wrenched open the passenger car door, his face twisted with anger. "Out. You fuckin' drive. Goddam fuckin' screw-up."

Rita shuffled over to the driver's seat, gripping the steering wheel, "Where to?"

"Fuckin' Lincoln High and don't stop for lights."

Chapter 26

Vinnie leaned back in the car seat staring at the glove compartment. "Do you know the director Luis Buñuel's quote on truth?"

Rita replied, "Nope, never did film."

"Well, it fits this case."

"Huh?"

"Buñuel said, 'I would give my life for a man who is looking for the truth. But I would gladly kill a man who thinks he has found the truth.' I just told Greg Fine that Judith McArthur knows the truth about his daughter."

The car sped along the main boulevard, yet to Vinnie it seemed like they were crawling. He urged Rita to drive faster as he watched them speed past local shops and houses. With some fidgeting on his cell phone he reached Blanca at the BIG office, his voice frantic as he requested she call an emergency meeting at Lincoln High. "Yes now. Otherwise it wouldn't be a fuckin' emergency." He turned off his cell phone.

Doris met Vinnie and Rita with a curt hello, then her hand gestured for them to enter the vice principal's office. Vinnie thought they had walked in on a congregational meeting, Mrs. Judith McArthur standing in front of her desk flanked by two men.

"Come in. You're Vincent Briggs and this is the new Mrs. Ricardo?"

"Rita Light."

"And I presume Mrs. Lucy Ricardo was the person who asked for this so-called emergency meeting?" No one extended hands for handshakes nor were smiles proffered. A cursory introduction identified the two men as the principal on her left and head of security on her right.

"Well, Mr. Briggs, you have our attention." Judith McArthur's face had a red tinge.

Vinnie's cheekbones pulled upward, jaw jutted, tongue clicked while turning back and forth between the principal and school security officer. The twenty-minutes exposé left the vice principal ashen. The security officer, a tall, heavy man with a smoker's rasp, spoke first. "I'll notify the police and drive Judith home."

"Nonsense, Bill, I'll drive myself. Nothing is going to happen in a few hours."

"I advise against it," said Bill, who handed Vinnie his card: Bill Crueller, Head of Security, Lincoln High. Vinnie smiled, fingering the card. *Is it Crul-ler, like the donut, or Cruel-er? Either way it was ironic for an ex-cop.*

No amount of cajoling changed Judith McArthur's mind about being escorted home.

In the car, Vinnie behind the wheel, he told Rita they would follow the vice principal. He tailed her Ford Taurus until she entered her driveway. Vinnie thought he saw a white van at the street end and pressed the gas pedal. A bicycle darted from a driveway requiring a sudden stop. A parent screamed, "Slow the fuck down! You'll kill one of our kids. It's a residential neighborhood, asshole!"

By the time Vinnie reached the intersection the van had vanished. After scouring a few blocks, Vinnie spied a deli and double-parked outside. Rita held the takeout unopened until they were parked at the end of Mrs. McArthur's street.

Finishing up the remains of his Italian sub, Vinnie leaned across Rita to fish a waste bag from the glove compartment and she lifted her salad to the car roof, partially blocking her view. Street lighting punctuated the darkness, tree shadows reaching out across the road. A mouthful of lettuce made Rita stumble over her words, but the noise was sufficient for Vinnie to sit up.

Mrs. McArthur's Taurus reversed from the driveway and drove by. Vinnie executed a three-point turn, speeding to catch up with her, unconcerned about kiddies playing as the hour meant they were probably encamped indoors snuggling up to TVs and video games.

The Taurus parked three hundred feet from the entrance to a mega store so large it was visible from aircraft at cruising altitude. Mrs. McArthur fox-trotted her way to the entrance. Vinnie searched for a parking location near the front, while Rita's eyes were glued to the store's main and only entrance. Pulling into an empty bay, Vinnie made an abrupt stop at a rapping on the side window.

"This is reserved," a young pre-teen with an official store blazer said to Vinnie.

Vinnie lowered his window. "I don't see a disabled sign."

"Not disabled, but for parents with young children. You know, with strollers. See?" said the kid, pointing at a sign. He looked like he was waiting for puberty to pop any moment, but he spoke like a thirty-year veteran cop. His finger pointed again at the sign indicating the reserved spaces. Vinnie squinted at the faded lettering on the tarmac identifying the bay was intended for parents with young children.

"Needs a fresh paint job."

"You blind? If so, use a disabled spot," the boy said in a high soprano and walked away. With restraint, Vinnie kept his thoughts private, and reversed the car, avoiding making tread marks on the kid's feet. Rita spied Mrs. McArthur returning to her car. Vinnie followed the parallel lane, only blocked by the same falsetto teen pushing a train of carts while retrieving another from a woman holding an infant in her arms. "Thank you, mam. Much appreciated."

"Could she even hear him or is his voice pitch only audible to dogs?" Vinnie shouted.

Rita patted Vinnie's shoulder. "You'll only make it worse."

By the time they reached the exit Judith McArthur was back on the main street. Vinnie gunned the car, nearly colliding with another attempting to edge him out. "Fuckin' Jersey drivers!" he screamed.

Rita focused on the Taurus's taillights, observing the car turn into a nondescript strip mall. The ten store facades were identical except for the garish signs hanging above. Judith McArthur entered a wine shop with a cute, pretentious name. "She'll need plenty to keep her calm, won't she?"

Vinnie drove by the front to park outside a shop with doodads of dubious value advertised as "indispensable quality items at discount prices."

"Why are we hiding from Judith?" Rita asked.

"Not her. Greg Fine. If we can photograph him near her we strengthen our case." Vinnie pointed to his camera on the back seat, which Rita brought to the front. Vinnie adjusted the telephoto lens setting.

"Why are you so sure he's following her?"

"I just am."

"Uh-huh. And let's say you're right. What if he attacks?"

"That's where you apply your kung fu and muscles while I snap pics." He smiled like a cat passing a chained dog.

Five minutes later Judith McArthur exited the shop with a large brown bag in her arms. An SUV stopped in front of Vinnie and Rita, blocking their view. A passenger door swung open, a woman stepping out, the driver saying, "I'll fill it up and be back by the time you're done."

"Sure, hon. I won't be long, just something for Sharon's kid's engagement shower." The large woman entered the fine-quality shopping establishment.

As the SUV pulled away, Vinnie and Rita could not see Mrs. McArthur. They looked at the Taurus to see if the interior light brightened or the taillights glowed. After two seconds Vinnie and Rita were out of the car and trotting in opposite directions.

Rita moved toward the end of the urban scrub. She saw a brown bag, a shattered wine bottle, glass and wine pooling on the sidewalk, and a discarded woman's handbag. She called out and Vinnie changed direction to join her. They ran toward a chain-link fence whose main function was to imprison overgrown shrubs, saplings, and tall weeds, and to trap strewn litter. The fence was no barrier to teenagers that had cut the links for easy access into a discreet nighttime place for sex and drugs.

Passing through the opening, Rita walked along the narrow passage with the aid of her cell phone's flashlight. Vinnie searched nearby vegetation. Her shout brought him running and stumbling over the uneven dirt pathway.

Rita held Judith McArthur's wrist with one hand, her other holding the phone. "A woman's been attacked and is unconscious."

Vinnie moved along the footpath to see a man leap a fence at the end. He pursued, instantly crashing to his knees when he tripped on an exposed tree root. By the time he was standing again the man was gone, lost among a small warehouse gumbo beyond a commercial railroad track. He returned to Rita and Mrs. McArthur.

"Anything?" Rita was lying next to Judith McArthur, who was underneath Rita's jacket. Vinnie placed his coat on top of Rita's.

"No. And her?" He pointed to Mrs. McArthur on the ground.

"She's unconscious but breathing and has a pulse. Bruised and concussed for sure, possibly with a cranial fracture and other bones broken. Let's wait to hear from the paramedics."

The diagnosis impressed Vinnie. Ben had said Rita's martial arts training included a modicum of medical knowledge and lots about human anatomy. Vinnie gave a half-smile.

Rita pointed along the path. "I surprised him. He had time for one blow." She handed Vinnie a cloth bag. "This was over her head so may have cushioned the initial blow. He might have been planning to take her elsewhere, to torture her and inflict greater damage than on the others." Rita paused. "Did you find the weapon?"

"No, it's too dark. Leave it to the cops so we don't get blamed for destroying the crime scene."

The paramedics talked to Mrs. McArthur when she regained consciousness. Before they entombed her in the ambulance, she turned to Vinnie and asked him to deliver the package from the megastore to her husband: his medication.

On their arrival at the McArthur residence, a patrol officer blocked Vinnie and Rita's entry until ordered to let them pass. A detective greeted them in the drive. He took the medication and handed it to another officer to take to Mr. McArthur in the upstairs master bedroom. Vinnie and Rita followed the detective into the living room.

"What clued you into Mrs. McArthur's attack?" The detective listed sideways, with his elbow resting on the fireplace mantel. Vinnie thought he looked Poirot-ish, except he had no mustache and the Jersey accent ruined the effect.

Vinnie recapped the events surrounding his Greg Fine interview and the emergency school meeting a few hours ago. He then ventured a smug opinion on New Jersey's Criminal Investigative Unit's bupkis investigation, which produced a short-lived grin from the detective. *Yes, a small waxed mustache and he'd be fuckin' Poirot.* Vinnie said he knew things were bad when he deduced Greg Fine's motive.

The detective glanced at his notes, "The owner of Fine Flowers, right?"

"I know it," said the detective's partner, sitting upright to the side of the fireplace. They were the first words he had spoken since they arrived. Zero Poirot, all Jersey cop. "He did the flowers for my father-in-law's funeral. Good job."

Vinnie continued with his theory but Poirot walked out of the room, and Vinnie and Rita followed without instruction. At the front door the detective pointed his pen out to the street, "We'll post a patrol car as an extra precaution."

"Will you question Greg Fine?" Poirot and Jersey walked away without answering Vinnie, who overheard Jersey say, "Fucking amateurs. Like they need to tell us what to do. Still, we might get free flowers for the wives. Ha ha ha."

Funny guy, thought Vinnie, *a real riot*. He turned to Rita. "We amateurs will also go for a bouquet—Fine but not free flowers I think."

Chapter 27

By late morning Vinnie and Rita were in the car on the New Jersey side of the Hudson. Vinnie complained, again, about the toll cost, calling it "highway robbery." With the amount he had paid crossing the Hudson in the last month he felt he should be a bridge shareholder.

"Our first stop will be to visit Richard McArthur before catching up with Greg Fine."

"Won't he be at the hospital with Judith?" Rita was chewing a protein bar.

"She was kept in overnight but released this morning." Vinnie pointed to Rita's snack. "Those things aren't healthy, you know. I read about them in a *Times* science article."

"What?" Rita bit into her protein bar as Vinnie shrugged.

Mr. McArthur was a tall, slender, frail man, older than his wife. He had a full white head of hair and trimmed beard. He wasn't what Vinnie or Rita expected.

"So, you retired a few years ago?" Vinnie was holding the tea that Mr. McArthur had made.

"Repeat, please." Mr. McArthur cupped one hand over his ear.

Vinnie said it again, louder.

"I wish. No, I retired eighteen years ago. I'm much older than Judith. Second marriage for me after my first wife died."

Vinnie turned to Rita and whispered, "Still not too badly off for an old codger, except his hearing." Rita tried to stifle her smile. Vinnie faced Mr. McArthur, voice again at a near shout. "Why did your wife go out after being warned?"

Waiting for the response, Vinnie's lips moved as if aiding Mr. McArthur to form words but the result was a series of short sputters from the old man, and nothing understandable. Vinnie looked to the window—*we'll be here until midsummer.* He rephrased his obviously overly complicated question, but mid-sentence he heard Mr. McArthur's voice.

"My fault..." His lips were on the verge of saying more.

Vinnie and Rita counted the checker patterns on the Oriental rug.

"I don't drive anymore, not with my vision. I have my medication at the Stop-N-Shop pharmacy. They stay open late, which makes it convenient but too far for me to walk from here. We had a local pharmacy a few blocks away, but they're long gone. Like the dodo."

The story dribbled out. Judith went to retrieve her husband's medicine. She also wanted her bottles of Umbrian Montepulciano that was carried by the specialty wine shop Vin-a-Go, and unavailable in the Stop-N-Shop liquor department. "Small place with better prices on brand names too, if you can believe that." Mr. McArthur's lecture wandered, a sermon on differences between the two stores' wine stock that expanded into general retail marketing strategies.

Vinnie coughed into his fist.

"And how's your wife? When do you think we could talk to her?" Vinnie had made the same request on entering the house, but Mr. McArthur either had not heard or had ignored the question, bringing the guests into the living room.

Mr. McArthur's answer was to describe his wife's mugging the previous night. "Lucky some fella came along and scared off her attacker."

Rita repeated Vinnie's question. "Can we visit Judith?"

"Oh, sure. She's much better now," he said, pointing to the ceiling. "She's upstairs in the bedroom reading. The doctors told her to take it easy but to sit up and walk around every hour or so. Do you want to talk to her?"

Vinnie turned again to Rita. "I guess Judith recovered in the forty minutes we've been here."

They entered the large master bedroom, a room Vinnie estimated to be thirty by forty feet, complete with high-end Scandinavian furniture that was definitely not IKEA. The room appeared classic nineteenth-century boudoir. Judith McArthur sat in a swivel chair at a small table, with a lamp and a teapot and cup beside her. Next to her chair was a two-seat divan. A third chair was placed to the right of a king-size bed on the other side of the room. She pointed to the divan, Vinnie took a seat and Rita stood behind expecting Mr. McArthur to take the other, but he sat in the remote chair, a perfect fit as if molded for his body. Vinnie looked for a microphone and loudspeaker system if Judith planned on communicating with her husband.

"These nice people... uh, what were your names again?" As Mr. McArthur spoke his hands shook, and his breath was short after the climb up the stairs.

"It's okay dear, I know who they are. You should go downstairs and relax." Judith's voice was at full volume.

Rita sat next to Vinnie. The vice principal thanked them for saving her life. Vinnie did not acknowledge the gratitude, his response a bulldog growl. "We warned you. Why did you go out?"

"My husband needed his medication, and I wanted my special wine since I would be home for a full week—precautionary measures imposed upon me. I thought nothing would happen so soon. Actually, I doubted anything would happen at all." Judith McArthur looked like she had just returned from combat in Afghanistan: head bandaged, eyes, nose, and chin shades of purple, green, and yellow, cheeks puffy, and one arm in a cast. Her authoritarian tone was also absent.

With measured cadence, Rita asked, "Did you recognize your assailant?"

"No."

"Anything familiar?" Rita suggested height or footwear or distinctive clothing, or something about his voice or mannerisms.

"The police already asked me these questions. Nothing. I'm sorry, but it's all a blur. The doctor says it's a temporary memory loss from being knocked unconscious."

Vinnie rubbed at his face. "How'd the attacker know you'd go out? Did he have an idea of your schedule maybe?"

This peculiarity had bothered Vinnie all night. How could Greg Fine know? Of course, there was no direct evidence that Fine actually was the attacker, but Vinnie was certain of it. He had hoped Judith McArthur recognized the person who assaulted her—something to go beyond circumstance and Vinnie's inference based on Greg Fine's reaction to learning of his mistaking McArthur for McCarthy.

"Richard didn't realize he was out of medicine. The pharmacy left a text message on our phone and he made a note on the pad." Mrs. McArthur paused seeing the twist to Vinnie's head. "Oh, his hearing. We have a modified hearing inductor phone with all the advanced gadgetry so he can make calls and receive texts too. Quite marvelous these modern devices. Same on his cell. But not much we can do with the onset of dementia, as you must have noticed."

"What time did you read the notepad message?" Rita used Vinnie's advice to be methodical in the follow-up questions.

"I always check for messages as soon as I come home but this time I must have missed it, upset by what you said. Not the threat, which I didn't believe—" She paused, sadness enveloped her bruised eyes, mouth twisting. "I am so sorry for Judy McCarthy. I mean, who would have thought..." Her voice trailed off. Vinnie started to answer but Rita gripped his arm to stop him from speaking.

Mrs. McArthur took a sip from the teacup. "I would have missed the message completely if the principal had not called to check up on me. He insisted I take the week off. After his call I saw the message on the pad."

***

"Fuckin' unbelievable," said Vinnie to Blanca's report after she had checked with the pharmacy about Mr. McArthur's prescription refill.

With the cell on speaker, Rita posed her question before Vinnie could curse a few more times. "You mean anyone can call a pharmacy and ask for a prescription refill?"

"Yes, if you have the address and prescription details."

"That's all you need?" said Vinnie, sounding doubtful.

Blanca's response was inpatient. "Vinnie, you of all people. The man has dementia and lost his pills. Why wouldn't the pharmacist refill the prescription?"

"Still—"

"Still what? It's not rocket science. Greg Fine worked out the details after you had gone. Maybe a visit to the McArthur home knowing Judith was at school. With a pretense, Mr. McArthur allows him into the house, Fine uses the bathroom and obtains the pharmacy details from a medicine bottle. I don't know exactly, but it would be easy to come up with a method."

Vinnie and Blanca dived into their devil's advocate roles, each pushing the other to flesh out ideas. "Then what?" They didn't take long to come up with a few plausible ways to get a prescription filled, and knowing the pharmacist would leave a text when the prescription was ready for pickup, the message Mr. McArthur copied to the notepad so that his wife could collect it for him.

The call ended, but fifteen minutes later Blanca was on the phone again. She had impersonated Judith McArthur to the pharmacy and had confirmation of the number of remaining refills using the number Vinnie had read off thanks to the medical details provided by Mrs. McArthur. The pharmacist stopped talking when Blanca asked the date of the last pickup since Mrs. McArthur had signed for the medication just twenty-four hours before—the person on the end of the line would have known that fact if she were Judith McArthur.

Blanca concluded her report. Vinnie looked to Rita. "If I had not bothered providing the case details during the school meeting, Judith McArthur would have been home early, talked to the pharmacist, and been alerted to a problem. Is this my fault?"

Rita reached to take Vinnie's arm, careful not to shake it as he drove. "I tell the women in my self-defense class never to blame themselves for being attacked. The victim does not cause the problem. Blame the attacker, not the victim. Now let's visit Fine, and this time I'm coming in, *capisce?*" which Rita pronounced "ka-pee-shy." Vinnie's eyebrows rose. "*Brava.* Now you can learn to say 'ciao, baby' to Greg Fine."

Chapter 28

The front entrance to the Fine Flowers Shop was locked, the interior dark. Vinnie's forehead leaned on the large glass window of the front door, his hands cupped around his eyes as if giving him X-ray vision. He called out to Greg Fine's ghost, "Fuckin' show yourself." Vinnie brooded. *Too fuckin' late.* The entrance door sign was clear: the florist shop was closed for one week to reopen under new management. After two minutes' waiting, Vinnie gave up attempting to conjure Greg Fine. Dispirited, he dragged himself back to his parked car.

Rita sprinted from the rear of the shop. She called Vinnie's name while running, but had no response. He was bending into his car's passenger door, reaching for a water bottle from the center console. Rita startled him by tapping his shoulder.

"Wait," she said.

"Huh?"

"I saw someone I recognized. She's over there." Rita pointed to a car parked down the block. She ran ahead, not waiting for Vinnie.

The pleasant woman in her mid-forties was unlocking a Prius when she turned to face Rita, her hand extended. They had exchanged a few words by the time Vinnie sauntered over.

"Liz, right? This is my partner Vinnie Briggs." Vinnie extended his hand. "Vinnie, did you meet Liz when you made your last floral order, that lovely bouquet you gave me? Well, you'll never guess, Liz is the new owner of Fine Flowers."

Vinnie's jaw went from wide open to gaping chasm. Not just from the news, but Rita's spontaneous and flawless creation of a fictitious backstory.

"When did this happen?" He was looking at Liz, his hand outstretched to greet her.

"Well, it was sudden, but not entirely unplanned. We've kept it quiet. Greg, I mean Mr. Fine," she paused with a giggle, "we all call him Greg. He insists. Anyway, he's wanted this for about six months." Liz gave more details than either Rita or Vinnie wanted to hear about Greg Fine's preparation, the paperwork, the secrecy, and sudden action—she had no explanation for the rapidity of the sale, but assumed it was for business reasons. She gave short chuckles with each sentence even though nothing she said was particularly funny. She looked around, almost as if they were being watched. "I don't blame him for wanting out, not after what he's been through."

Vinnie nodded his agreement, not knowing what he agreed with. Rita turned to him, "Isn't this good news for Liz?" She turned to Liz. "I guess you must like flowers?"

"Yes. I've been with Greg for fifteen years. I started just after college. A liberal arts major, you know, the one with the unemployable esthetic degree." Liz chuckled again. Her eyes were bright, the kind people describe as buttons.

"So, you were able to buy out Mr. Fine?"

"Oh, heavens no. Not exactly. Greg is such a good and generous man. He lent me a personal loan to show the bank I had sufficient initial capital, then he co-signed as guarantor. God knows I couldn't have done this without his help. A truly wonderful man."

Sure, as murderers go he's a real fuckin' sweetheart. Vinnie's face was snarling as more thoughts entered his mind. He felt Rita's arm rest on his shoulder, and he spoke like he had a toothpick between his teeth. "I bet you deserve it. Congratulations. Where is Mr. Fine now?"

"Probably packing. Greg said he was planning a little vacation. Off somewhere warm and sunny to relax, that sort of thing. He deserves it. He often stayed after the store closed and would open before any of us arrived. I guess that's my job now!"

Houses blurred past as Vinnie took curves as if on the Indianapolis 500, shortening the time to Greg Fine's home by fifteen minutes. He parked halfway along the driveway near the front entrance. The driveway was so long that Vinnie expected a tollbooth at the four-car garage that looked like a carriage house with a second floor above. The house was an old-style brick building, built circa 1925, and had eight chimneys with a modern addition at the rear big enough for the annual Macy's Spring Flower Show. Vinnie thought the plot at least fifteen acres, an extensive woodland in the rear and a front lawn that could double for a par nine golf course.

He rang the front doorbell five times. Rita shook her head. "Uh, Vinnie, I don't think he's home."

"Fuckin' bastard. We need to check the airport. Alert the police."

"And say what? 'Someone we're pretty sure is a murderer probably attacked Judith McArthur last night. We have no proof, but he may have boarded an airplane going *somewhere*. Arrest him and don't worry about the missing evidence'—you think that covers it?"

Vinnie walked around the side of the house to the rear, up the back entrance's five steps to a large porch veranda, then returned to the front, a journey of a few minutes. He carried with him a long box and gave Rita a Fine Flowers card hand-addressed as: "TO Mr. V. Briggs." Inside the box were twelve yellow roses with one white. Rita read out loud:

Congratulations, Mr. Briggs. You are a good detective. I would recommend you to my friends if I were there. I've retired at fifty-three, early but necessary. I plan to travel. I'm not good with postcards and won't be writing 'wish you were here.' Ha ha. Best of luck. And you can tell Mrs. McArthur for now she's <u>Fine</u>. I strongly recommend Mrs. M. retire early for her own safety.

GF

***

At the BIG office the team huddled while Vinnie grumbled. "He's fuckin' getting away with it. And we don't know all the facts or even all the victims. We messed up."

Rita piped up, "No, we didn't. We saved Judith McArthur."

"And did she deserve to be saved?" Vinnie closed his eyes. "I didn't mean that. Of course she did. It's not our job to act as a jury and judge. We investigate and let others decide on justice." Vinnie paused. *Is that true? Do we leave it to others? Have I?*

Blanca tapped her bare feet with her hands rested on her thighs. "It's over. Nothing more we can do except prepare a report for our client Roger Bryant."

Vinnie looked around the room. "Do you think he'll be satisfied knowing he was right and his wife's murder and Emily Dingle's were connected? Or more upset knowing bullying by his son and Brett Dingle resulted in their mothers' deaths?"

"Doesn't matter either way," Blanca said as she sat in front of her computer. "Once we send the report over, we've done what he asked. Then we're finished."

"No." Rita stood, her arm waving in front of her. "Two more people need to know and I should be the one to tell them."

***

He hesitated before stepping aside for Rita to enter his home. Glen's arms hung down to his knees, like an ape. He even grunted as she walked in. Rita thought the King Kong act was getting boring. His sneer left her in no doubt that had he been Kong holding her atop the one-hundred-two-storied Empire State Building he would have happily tossed her over the side. There was no offer of a drink and he grudgingly allowed her to sit.

"I won't take long but there's something you need to know."

"Damn right you won't be long. And why should I believe a goddam word you say?"

"Because I told you I never meant to hurt you—" Glen's bark interrupted Rita but she continued, her voice irritated. "And I told you our purpose was to find out who killed Emily. I'm here to tell you everything we know."

The visit lasted an hour, prolonged by Glen's many interruptions. He admitted Brett's bullying, yet repeated that Ken Bryant played the primary role. He had been disgusted that Roger Bryant had paid his share of the Dellarosa settlement and then lorded it over him, but the deal depended on both parties paying. They never spoke after, not for legal reasons but because of the humiliation he felt and Roger's resentment. Both were angry with their sons, and the protection afforded because of their mothers' positions at Lincoln High.

"But you spoke to Roger at the hospital. Meeting you was the reason he hired us."

A small smile found a way to Glen's lips and his eyes had the sparkle that had first attracted her to him. His voice became less tense. "The big events, the real tragedies make all else trivial. We both lost our wives to brutal murders. Who cares now about the money? I don't and I'll bet Roger doesn't either. I'm left to raise Brett alone, and I've made a mess of that." He nodded his head while looking at her.

If she thought he wouldn't freak out she would have hugged him. More than hugged. Comforted him. Had sex with him, not erotic sex, but love, to show him she cared.

Holding open the front door, Glen looked down on Rita. "And I do believe you now but it won't work. I have to consider Brett. His mother's death and what happened that night has changed him. This won't help, but I have to tell him." He stopped, his voice choking. "Goodbye, Rita." Glen leaned over and kissed her cheek, whispering, "God, I loved you so much." His voice cracked and the door quickly closed.

Rita's tears soaked her face as she drove away.

***

"Please, come in." Jim McCarthy's wide smile brightened the doorway. Rita entered the condo, her sloping shoulders burdened with her task. She slumped in the chair while he prepared them herbal tea.

He'll wish it was poison after he hears what I have to say, Rita thought. "It seems better to talk in person, instead of phone or email." She stopped. "I don't know why, but it just does."

"Absolutely. I enjoyed your company last time." Jim's short laugh had a soothing quality. "That sounds pushy, doesn't it? I hope you're not offended." He flashed a smile, glistening teeth set in a perfect face, his head crowned by thick lush hair.

"Not at all." Rita rubbed her moist palms together. She brought the teacup to her mouth but before sipping replaced it back on the table. A tremor developed in her hand; her years of yoga were no use in steadying her nerves. She forced a smile half as wide as his.

"This won't be easy for you to hear, but I think it may help." She stared, breathing through her nostrils, lips curled inward. She sighed before speaking.

As with Glen, her intended short explanation stretched to an hour. Jim interrupted as much as Glen, but his questions were different, no worry about his culpability in a cover-up. He understood confusing his wife's name with Judith McArthur, but not Greg Fine's failure to check facts. With his face buried in his hands and truth's weight loaded on to him, Jim McCarthy broke. "God, that sounds awful. Forgive me. I don't mean I want Mrs. McArthur to have died in place of Judy. I'm sorry. I'm..." His hands remained over his face, the wedding ring reflecting sunlight. His weeping escalated into anguished sobs.

Rita moved next to Jim, her arm around his shoulders. "It's okay. I know what you mean. Don't do this to yourself."

His sobbing subsided. "That Judy died because of mistaken identity... I can't find comfort. It feels worse somehow. Pointless."

"No. That was not my intention. Please, Jim, I thought you'd want to know."

Rita tightened her hold. Now was the time to keep quiet. She held Jim, pulling his head to her bosom, allowed his sobs to drench her blouse. Neither spoke. As the minutes passed the sobbing gradually subsided again, and Jim moved to rest his cheek on Rita's shoulder. "I miss her. I... so much..."

"Yes and..." Rita stopped herself, reluctant to offer advice on how he should act or feel. *Keep quiet. First rule.*

Jim looked up at Rita, their faces inches apart. He leaned in to Rita's tilting head, the distance between lips closing. She felt his soft breath brush her lips. Rita's head moved forward until her lips touched his. His strong arms wrapped around her shoulders, and hers folded underneath his ribcage. They moored each other, melding body and soul. Rita called out for a dove, which confused Jim. He didn't ask for explanation, too amazed as she shed her clothes, stood naked before him, then straddled his lap.

In two hours Rita restored Jim McCarthy's life, and hoped it would last more than one afternoon. She wanted him to wake, not to forget Judy, but not remain in a life of morose pity. She didn't love him, not like Glen. But she told Jim she would voluntarily return anytime, without hesitation, and with no commitment. "You've got my number. But you have to decide what to do next. Like you told me, no one can tell you how to feel or act. But I'll provide whatever you need from me. *Whatever you need.* Understand?"

Jim looked up from the bed where he sprawled naked, sweat glistening on his body, a smile that barely fitted his face. "Yes, I understand."

Chapter 29

One Month Later

Blanca's nose turned up, as if a putrid mess had been dumped on her desk. The cause of her upset was a long white box with a dozen short-stem yellow roses and a single white. She handed Vinnie the small card.

Vinnie stared at the card addressed to Blanca. "Secret admirer?"

"Funny. Read it. They're meant for you."

Vinnie looked again at the small envelope. "Um, name says Blanca Santos."

"*Tonto.* Just read."

The note suggested Blanca was owed a weekend getaway, and the flowers were to decorate her room. Vinnie turned the card over: blank. "So?"

"Like I said, they're for you." Blanca's arms folded.

"How so? You want me to book a room at the Marriott for you, is that it?"

"Sometimes you are so dense. I mean you take this note to the Jersey State Police and the FBI." Blanca lifted the flowers, pushing them into Vinnie's chest. "And get rid of them. Throw them in the river. I don't care."

Vinnie took the box saying he'd toss them in the building dumpster, but Rita objected. She thought they might be important for the police.

The flowers rested on the car's back seat, and Rita acted the demur passenger to Vinnie's tough-guy chauffeuring. His complaining about the flowers stopped on entering the New Jersey toll plaza of the Lincoln Tunnel, where he switched to speaking ill of the Garden State.

The two BIG investigators entered single-file into the New Jersey Violent Criminal Apprehension Program office, Rita carrying the florist box, long enough to conceal a sawn-off shotgun. Two entrance guards stared at Rita as she passed through security scanners, one making a gruff demand that the box be opened for inspection. "Nice bunch," said one officer, with an ambiguous hand gesture that could have referenced either the flowers or Rita's assets. She made a less ambiguous return gesture that the security guard should shove a rose up his ass. Vinnie quickly intervened, flashing his NJ PI license gained for this case; that had been a lot of hassle to acquire. Even his New York license had been problematic, given his criminal arrest history but lack of convictions. If not for the San Francisco DA and SFPD's recommendation and citation of Vinnie's aid in solving multiple homicides, his application would be resting in an NYC landfill.

"Mr. Briggs and Ms. Light, you say you have been working on a private multiple homicide investigation for a few months? Why did you wait to notify us?" asked the NJ lieutenant, coordinator for the State's homicide units.

Vinnie scoffed, "This, for starters." Vinnie passed the note to the lieutenant. Two fat fingers attached to an enormous mitt-sized hand delicately took the envelope. He kept his eyes fixed on Vinnie and only turned his head when Rita placed the flower box on his desk. Adjusting his reading glasses, the lieutenant read the note, and like Vinnie he then turned it over to inspect the reverse.

"And what's this mean?"

For fifteen minutes Vinnie recapped his theory and the background to each murder victim. He thought the lieutenant looked bored hearing about Dan Livorno's outlier analysis. Vinnie smiled a few times, yet the lieutenant's facial expression remained unchanged; only a series of small nods implied either approval or comprehension but Vinnie was unsure which.

As he finished, the lieutenant said, "We find outliers can be key to solving difficult cases, those that fall outside the statistical norm."

Fuckin' A, thought Vinnie as his smile broadened, then vanished just as fast as the lieutenant continued, "Good you followed up, but I don't understand the meaning of this note. And why not share this with Division B that handles Bergen County? And local police?"

Pursing his lips, Vinnie shrugged. "We tried, but no one was interested. They said the facts did not support an investigation. They changed their minds after Judith McArthur's attack, but it was too little, too late. These flowers are more proof." Vinnie stopped to look at the box on the desk.

With his facial expression unchanged, but a slight irritation in his voice, the lieutenant said, "Explain."

"We looked into the FTD order sent to our BIG office. They came from Greg Fine."

"But neither Fine Flowers nor Greg Fine's name appear anywhere."

Vinnie's eyebrows lowered to form deep creases on his forehead. "There is no doubt." The lieutenant's arms moved wide, his hands rose upward, and lips pursed asking the unspoken question: Where's the proof?

"We checked." Vinnie's throat raked the words. He skipped the means by which Blanca illegally accessed the FTD database, just cited her findings. "The flowers arrived from a local Manhattan florist but the FTD order originated from Fine Flowers. The new owner of Fine Flowers confirmed the order did not originate at one of the Fine shops, but—and here's the kicker—was placed after hours with the Fine FTD link. Only one person other than the current owner can access that code outside the store's direct link."

Leaning back in his chair, the lieutenant held up the single white rose. "And the colors are significant?"

Rita turned to Vinnie sporting her I-told-you-so smile then looked into the lieutenant's eyes. "Yes, a dozen yellow roses and a single white matches the order we had delivered to the Marriott. Here's the clincher: this combination is Greg Fine's signature bouquet. We can give you several examples that you can confirm."

Without waiting for Rita to finish, Vinnie said, "The flower combination is no outlier."

The lieutenant's face elongated and his lips parted a sliver to say, "We'll look into it."

***

Present Day

Two months after the Trenton visit, a letter marked "personal" arrived for Vinnie at BIG. Blanca handed the open letter to Vinnie as he walked into the office.

"You won't believe this."

Taking the letter, Vinnie examined the airmail envelope franked with a Brazilian stamp. "It says personal."

"I assumed that includes me."

"Oh right. Care to share my bed with Ben? That's personal too."

"Ben yes. You, not so much."

Vinnie was already on to the second paragraph.

"Quite something, isn't it?" Blanca batted her eyelashes.

"Fuckin' unbelievable."

Rita arrived an hour later. Blanca handed her the letter and she read it out loud.

Mr. Briggs,

You had most of it right. I congratulate you on surpassing both the cops and FBI. As a mark of my esteem, my gift is to save you time pursuing me, if indeed you still are. It won't take a master sleuth to deduce I'm in Brazil, but not for long.

As a return favor, I ask you express to Jim McCarthy my sincerest regret and deep sadness. I doubt he'll find solace. I would not. I can never forgive myself confusing two people so different. For that mistake I have retired—and I don't mean as a florist.

Which brings me to my next point. Mrs. McArthur is safe in her recent retirement—as I learned from the Internet. She does not deserve peace and should worry every day, but my vengeance is spent. Time has not lessened my grief for Dawn. It is up to you whether to inform Mrs. McArthur or let her stew. I know you found her as despicable as I did, another reason you have my admiration.

Rita stopped with Vinnie's outburst: "Unbelievable, isn't it? Just fuckin' unbelievable. He admires me. Well, I don't admire him."

"Hmm." Rita put the note down to her side. "You sure about that?"

Vinnie looked at his fingernails. He had said awful things about Judith McArthur and her complicity with two star athletes. Vinnie wanted to disagree with Rita but couldn't.

Rita continued reading.

> *Let me be clear on one point. Dawn's overdose was suicide, brought on by despair at Jessica Reinhardt's constant bullying.*

"That's probably true," said Vinnie, interrupting Rita.

> *Bob Reinhardt ignored my pleas. He was my only male victim because his wife was already dead. I chose an exploding bullet to eradicate his entire being, like Dawn.*

Rita finished by reading the rest of the letter to herself, a meandering tome on laws, school administrators, and future action. "It's all Pollyanna crap this, 'I would like to think my legacy will cause schools to enforce strong anti-social behavior policies to stop bullying.'" Rita read ahead, "except this bit makes some sense," and she read out loud:

If schools enforce strong anti-social behavior policies they can stop bullying. Winning seasons mean players get free passes from coaches, principals, and law enforcement. Four years of special treatment in high school plants the seed of entitlement. College and pro-teams nurture this seed into the arrogance of star stature, and the entitlement becomes the gateway to abuse, rape, and murder with impunity. High schools breed contempt for the law when bullying is overlooked.

"I agree, he's probably right, or almost." Vinnie looked at Blanca. "Do you worry if your kids don't make the team? Aren't the big boys in high school?

"I didn't until now. They have a few years before high school, but I'm worried." Blanca looked at her hands. "Both ways. If not popular athletes, will they be bullied? If they are, do they become the bullies?"

"Doesn't have to be that way." Rita placed her hand on Blanca's shoulder. "Not if we teach them to respect women and men." She paused, looking upward. "And women to respect each other by not supporting male chauvinists and sadists."

Vinnie took hold of the note from Rita. "Here's the kicker: Fine puts the burden on the mothers. Uses the mothers' deaths to message the kids."

Rita twisted her lips, sucking in her cheeks. "So Fine chose women not because they were easier prey but because he blames mothers more than fathers."

"Do you think he's right?" Vinnie looked to Blanca. "Do mothers have more influence than fathers over their children?"

With a sheepish smile, Blanca lifted her shoulders. "You tell me."

Shaking her head, Blanca said she despised Fine's approach, and his obscure way to give out a message. "Why not purchase TV ads or post online or tweet or anything? He has the money to do a blitz campaign."

"And speaking of money, read the last part," said Vinnie.

Enclosed is an offshore account containing five million dollars. I've put you on the account. I ask you to create a tax-exempt fund for scholarships, therapy, parent support, and legal fees that relate to bullying. Call the fund the Judy McCarthy Memorial Foundation with Jim McCarthy's permission. If he declines (he probably will), then call it the Dawn Fine Foundation. If you opt out, ask the new Fine Flowers proprietor to take on the task—she'll be confused, angry, and disappointed, which can't be helped. Details are with my attorney.

Neither you nor anyone else will hear from me again.

Sincerely,

Greg Fine

Rita placed the letter on the desk.

Vinnie stared at the murderer's letter as if it was a dog turd. He picked it up, sliding the edge between his index finger and thumb, feeling the paper's texture. This did not satisfy. Solving the case felt so wrong.

Rita whistled. "Do you think... I mean, is this a suicide note?"

Vinnie shrugged.

Blanca said, "We can only hope.

Did you love *Outlier Man*? Then you should read *Detour Man*[1] by Charles Puccia!

[2]

PI Vinnie Briggs has a new client.
Muscles from a fourth-dimension, yet a puny self-image. Timid but capable of crushing a person. Linked to bodies in the morgue.

Vinnie knows bodybuilder Gunter Hoffman developed his enormous size to keep at bay nightmares of his childhood nemesis, a menacing homeless guy with PTSD known as Detour Man. He's afraid of people, and lonely.

---

1. https://books2read.com/u/m2PzeR

2. https://books2read.com/u/m2PzeR

A random encounter with international terrorists puts Gunter on a path of mass murder. Vinnie, with co-investigator Rita Light, must prove Gunter's innocence using illegal methods, lying, and sex. Their actions risks innocent lives.

To win, Gunter must conquer his fear. Can he forget a regret while condemned to remember heartbreak?

Vinnie and Rita must save Gunter from becoming the Detour Man.

Read more at www.charlespuccia.com.

About the Author

Unscrupulous characters populate the Vinnie Briggs mystery-thriller series. Each book follows a theme: obsession, love/family, privilege, fear, and betrayal. The novels follow contemporary language and adult behaviors. Readers that like 18+ movies will enjoy these stories.

Read more at www.charlespuccia.com.